JUST DESERTS

And Lesser Punishments

By David T. Snyder

KLEENAN PRESS
Post Office Box 1213
Walled Lake, Michigan 48390-1213

Library of Congress Control Number 2009907145

Printed in the United States of America

ISBN 978-0-9745081-5-3

This book is dedicated

to the restoration of

civilized behavior, however

unlikely.

Chapter One

Frankie Bonner turned 14 in the late summer of 1942 when a desperate international conflict that would one day be called World War Two still had several years to go before the Allied forces – mainly the United States, Britain and Russia – would defeat the Axis nations, primarily Germany, Japan and Italy. Unable to foretell the future and with an intense desire to trade the boredom of public schooling for life on some distant battlefield, he feared the war would not last long enough for him to grow into it. "Rats," he often said to himself when this frustrating reality crossed his mind.

The teenager understood to some extent the events of that year, mainly news of one military disaster after another for the United States following the surprise Japanese attack on Pearl Harbor late in 1941. But his immaturity made it all but impossible to grasp the real threat to the nation that surrounded St. Louis, his hometown. He knew from radio reports and discussions with school friends about the Japanese conquest of the Philippine Islands in the spring, but he didn't know about the long death march in which 75,000 American and Filipino war prisoners were made to take from the Bataan Peninsula to squalid camps and the brutal treatment that killed many of them along the way.

Frankie was more focused on the escape in a small naval patrol boat from the Philippines by General Douglas MacArthur and his promise to one day return, a stirring enough oath that bolstered morale at home but did little to help those who were left in the hands of a brutal enemy.

The boy was vaguely aware the German Afrika Korps under General Rommel had taken Bengasi in Libya in January and by June would capture Tobruk and penetrate Egypt before its North African drive was stopped by the British 8th Army at El Alamein. These place names have since been burned into the consciousness of both students of military history and the seriously curious, but at the time made little impact on this near juvenile whose main occasional ambition was to kill a few Japanese and German soldiers without sustaining any material damage to himself.

Like other Americans who had been accustomed to a continuous barrage of bad war news, he was patriotically stirred by the first U.S. air raid in mid-April on the Japanese home islands. The raid was led by Lieutenant Colonel James Doolittle and was carried out with 16 Army Air Force bombers launched for the first and only time from a Navy aircraft carrier on a war-time mission. The planes bombed Tokyo and a variety of other Japanese cities and then most of the group made long flights to China where most of the crews either crash-landed or parachuted into friendly hands. All aircraft were lost on the mission and 11 crewmen were either killed or captured, but the crews of 13 planes were soon recovered and returned to the United States. Another crew that had gone down in the outer reaches of the Soviet Union was returned the next year.

Doolittle parachuted into a Chinese dung heap – which was probably more amusing in retrospect than it was at the time – but eventually found his way home with the help of friendly soldiers and others.

Frankie's birthday in August of 1942 coincided with the arrival in Russia of German troops at the Volga River immediately north of Stalingrad where an incredibly fierce battle would rage into the early months of the next year, leaving the city in ruins and hundreds of thousands dead on both sides. But the Russians – who had lost more than six million killed or captured soldiers before the battle for Stalingrad – had inflicted a crushing defeat on the German army and destroyed its invincible reputation.

One description of life for the soldiers and few remaining civilians in Stalingrad called it "an endless hell' of explosions, gunfire, screaming dive bombers, rockets, smoke, dust and rubble combined with hunger, exhaustion, fear and the smell of death. Frankie had no notion of this harsh reality and knew there was a war on mainly as a result of the endless war bond campaigns and the various drives to collect scrap metals, paper and even bacon grease to make munitions in the enormous production effort then gathering momentum. He knew, too, that gasoline had been rationed, but it made little difference to him or most of his friends. Their families had not been able to afford automobiles during the great economic depression of the 1930s and no new ones would be produced until after the war.

As it would for the duration, war dominated the home front news in 1942, but there were other events of lesser importance to distract the easily distracted mind of a 14-year-old boy. Early in the year, heavyweight boxing champion Joe Louis knocked out Buddy Baer in the first round of their fight, catching the challenger with a short right that spun him around 360 degrees. Baer – who stood almost six feet, seven inches and weighed 250 pounds – said later the only way he could have beaten Louis was "with a baseball bat." Louis went on to defend his heavyweight title, which he retained for almost 12 years, some 25 times. He had 68 wins – 54 by knockouts – and three losses, but his record would have been even more impressive had he not made an ill-advised comeback late in his career.

Frankie admired the black heavyweight champion but failed to notice there were no children of the fighter's kind in his public school or in the modest neighborhood where he lived. The city was in what had been a border state during the American Civil War, which meant it had retained into the 1940s the racist policies and attitudes of the south but in a more restrained and somewhat less noticeable way. There was only one black the boy knew personally, a big, muscled man who did maintenance and janitorial work for several of the six-family apartment buildings on his block. "White people," the man told Frankie, "were originally lepers, made that way by God for their sins." He passed that information along in a paternal manner, but the negative implications were clear to the boy even then. Frankie neither believed nor disbelieved the assertion, however, probably because it was made when he was still quite young and had not the least notion of lepers or the disease that made them that way.

Among other distractions from the war in 1942 was the death in January of Carole Lombard, a famous film star in her own right and the wife of another one, Clark Gable. She was among 22 passengers aboard a Los Angeles-bound Trans World Airlines flight that crashed

Into Table Mountain in Nevada's Potosi Range, leaving no survivors and providing her war-oriented public with an opportunity to mourn a civilian. Miss Lombard had boarded the plane in Indianapolis where she had participated in a successful war bond sale. The airliner had made a final refueling stop in Las Vegas early in the evening, and had crashed shortly after take-off on the final leg of its flight.

Carole Lombard was born Jane Alice Peters in Fort Wayne, Indiana in 1908, and went on to a film career in the 1920s and 30s that made the transition from silent to talking movies, something a number of actors with poor voices failed to accomplish. She was posthumously awarded the Medal of Honor by President Franklin Roosevelt as the first woman killed in the line of duty during the Second World War and before the conflict was over a Liberty ship was named for her. Carole Lombard now occupies a mausoleum at Forest Lawn cemetery in Glendale, California, next to Clark Gable, who joined her in 1960 when his time ran out. All this was a matter of great importance to the many thousands of Americans whose theater attendance made it possible for a select group of actors to live like Roman aristocracy, but it was a matter of absolutely no concern to Frankie Bonner whose interest in movies was restricted to the cheap western and other thrillers that were shown at Saturday matinees in those days. The theaters that displayed these movies smelled like a combination of old bananas and stale popcorn, an aroma that derived from the brown bag lunches the audience, mainly boys, brought with them and the stuff that was popped and sold for a nickel a bag in the lobbies.

At the time, Frankie and his peers were completely unaware of the forcible relocation of more than 100,000

Japanese-Americans, mainly from the west coast, to bleak internment camps further inland. President Roosevelt authorized the internment with an executive order that made it possible to establish zones from which those of Japanese ancestry were excluded, an area that covered the entire U.S. Pacific coast.

Anti-Japanese sentiments had long prevailed in California, where the great majority of immigrants from Japan had settled for years. Those racist notions along the west coast were amplified by the war with Japan, but these attitudes were less prevalent in other parts of the nation. There was a respected Japanese artist in Frankie's home town who taught at one of the universities and was asked to paint a large patriotic picture to promote war bond sales. The painting – which showed U.S. marines charging bravely up a hill into enemy gunfire – was installed in the main display window of a downtown department store, where it was seen by thousands of pedestrians and generally admired for its qualities. The artist, however, had slyly gained a measure of revenge by painting the marines with oriental eye folds, a detail that escaped the attention of almost everyone who rushed past the store window.

Early in 1942, Frankie understood imperfectly that Imperial Japan had been successful in its prosecution of the war, but he didn't quite grasp that this relatively small island nation had conquered nearly all of Southeast Asia. From the American point of view, there was a torrent of bad war news – broken occasionally by a positive event such as the Doolittle bombing raid – but there was also his school life and puberty which made the emerging breasts on some girls in his class a more immediate reality than the bloody activities on distant shores. The war had intruded on him to some extent, but his city was not under bombardment and young men from his neighborhood had not yet been maimed or killed in the long series of battles that would be fought before the war was won.

Although there was no clear winner on either side, the Battle of the Coral Sea on four days in May was probably a narrow victory for the Japanese navy. They lost one small aircraft carrier with a large one crippled while the American forces lost a large carrier and another sustained significant damage. But it was the first time a Japanese invasion force had been turned back, and it was an intimation of better things to come for the United States and its allies in the Pacific war.

It was also the first time in naval history in which ships on either side neither saw nor fired directly on the other. The battle was conducted mainly with dive and torpedo bombers operating from carriers, although the U.S. side did deploy land-based B-17s in an attack before the Army Air Force realized some time later that high-level bombing of moving naval targets was a futile enterprise.

In what is widely considered the most decisive battle of the Second World War, the Battle of Midway resulted in the effective destruction of Japan's naval strength and put the handwriting on the wall as far as the eventual outcome of the total conflict was concerned. Fought in June – only a month after the two navies met in the Coral Sea – the Japanese lost four irreplaceable aircraft carriers that had been considered essential to their Pacific campaign. They also lost hundreds of experienced crewman as well as the great offensive momentum they had gathered in the six months since the war had begun. In the battle, the United States lost the carrier Yorktown, which had been damaged in the

Coral Sea and quickly repaired in time to participate in the engagement off Midway Island. The vessel, disabled by Japanese aircraft, might have been towed in for repairs again had an enemy submarine not penetrated the American fleet and sunk the ailing carrier with two torpedoes. But the United States, unlike the Japanese, was able to replace its losses.

Frankie Bonner shared with friends in the elation of that first great victory, but soon turned his thoughts to summer vacation from school. He had just begun to work in those three months, and 1942 would be the last year in which he still had significant leisure to spend on various recreations. He spent many of the days at a public swimming pool or at the tennis facility in the city's great central park where the clay courts were often out of use following frequent summer rains. He owned a bicycle that gave him considerable mobility at a time when automobile traffic was naturally light as the result of gasoline rationing. And like other boys his age and before the suburbs spread miles from the core city, there were few places in the general area beyond the range of his light, multiple speed bike.

The distant war and its many effects on the home front were a matter of continuing concern to most American adults in those early months of the conflict, but the parents of children were also confronted each summer with a menacing prospect that had nothing to do with Japan or Germany. Infantile paralysis or Poliomyelitis – more commonly called polio – crippled thousands, mostly young children, until past the mid-point in the 20th century when effective vaccines were developed that all but eradicated the scourge in North America. This viral disease had crippled or killed for thousands of years, but didn't achieve epidemic dimensions until the late 1800s in Europe and the early 1900s in the United States. By the summer of 1942, fear of the disease – which years earlier had afflicted President Franklin Roosevelt – was palpable among many parents. They kept their children from public swimming pools where polio was thought to be spread, a prohibition that Frankie and many like him managed to circumvent in the interest of good times. The heavy smell of chlorine may have assured them of a pool's purity, despite the sure knowledge – confirmed by irregular warm currents in the water – that there were those among them too lazy or thoughtless to urinate in more appropriate places. In any case, Frankie and his kind had little interest or fear of bacterial or viral agents, and left those concerns along with the war to their parents.

Frankie Bonner was the only child of a city police detective father who was shot to death in the line of duty when the boy was 10, and a mother who subsequently went to work out of sheer necessity. The father, J.D. Bonner, had accidentally confronted three robbers as they emerged from a bank and had taken a bullet to the chest as he drew his service revolver. The dying officer managed to get off a single shot at the fleeing felons, which struck and killed one of them and instilled a sense of pride in the boy that remained with him for the rest of his life. At 10, he had been old enough to know and remember the father who had taken him to baseball games and given him, behind his mother's back, nickels for ice cream cones. The loss of this benevolent figure and the circumstances of his death gave Frankie a profound hatred for the criminal element in society that was far stronger than the natural distaste most honest citizens have for those who break the law. The boy came to believe that no retribution was too great for killers and robbers, although he submerged these feelings beneath an otherwise placid disposition for reasons he neither understood nor worried about.

Frankie's mother was a trained nurse who had given up the profession when she married in her mid-20s and resumed the career more than a decade later when her husband was killed. She was able to support herself and her son in modest comfort, which was made possible by the emergence of a war-time economy that displaced a long and generally miserable economic depression that had made hardship a way of life for millions. Through application and native aptitude for the work, Sally Bonner ascended the nursing hierarchy at a large local hospital where she soon established a reputation for competence and reliability.

Although she always made provisions for Frankie's meals and other necessities, his mother's demanding work schedule gave the boy a degree of independence most of his peers would not realize until they were several years older. Sally Bonner trusted her son to behave with prudence, which, of course, was a mistake, but one she was bound to make in the accommodation of her long and irregular work hours. Frankie lied to his mother with regularity about the hours he kept and the places he went, and did it partially to maintain the freedom he came to prize and partially to console the hard-working woman he loved. As a result, he came to believe early in life that the virtue in truth is, at least, somewhat over-rated.

"Yeah, mom," he said one morning not long after she arrived home from a tiring night shift assignment and he was leaving for school, "I did my homework and went to bed about nine." She didn't know he had waited for her anticipated eight o'clock phone call the previous night, assured her he was doing school work, and then gone out with confidence her needy patients would not allow time for a later call.

In 1942, a person – even one of Frankie's age – could roam most of the city's streets in relative safety. In his particular case, the attraction was a 15-year-old girl he had met one afternoon at the neighborhood drug store. Tall for his age, she had mistaken his size for someone a bit more mature and had lured him into the night streets with provocations he barely understood. He took her freedom to stay out at night for granted and gave little thought to this unusual circumstance. Actually, her situation was strikingly similar to his. She had a single, working parent and little adult supervision to restrain rampant hormonal urges. She sought a young man with similar inclinations, but didn't realize that Frankie barely understood the process.

"Do you have a condom?" she inquired as they walked together down the street one drizzly summer night. She had taken his hand captive and put it in her raincoat pocket where he could feel the upper reaches of her leg.

"I don't think so," he replied, wondering what she meant.

"A rubber," she said, clarifying the matter for this person who was beginning to reveal the rather significant extent of his ignorance.

"Oh," was the only thing he could think to say. He now understood her intention, but didn't know what to do about it. He neither had the item she sought nor knew what to do with it or where to go had he had one. "No," he admitted at last.

Frankie's experience with sex had been restricted to

the barely informative magazines on the subject he had shared with some of his friends and the completely misinformed discussions he had with these same boys. They had mostly ogled the younger teachers at their school, watching clandestinely for any indication of breasts when one of the women wore a snug sweater or anything else that stirred their lascivious natures. Frankie and his friends were on the cusp of sexual awareness, but had not quite reached that point on the night the young woman sought his services.

"Walk me home," she instructed once it was apparent he was not likely to take any initiative on his own. And since no other option occurred to him and his hand, held tightly by hers, was still in her coat pocket, he went wordlessly where she led him. He was aware, however, that she was massaging the interior of her thigh with his captive hand as they walked the few blocks to the apartment building where she lived. "Holy shit,' he thought as they entered the vestibule and she initiated a long kiss in which her little tongue darted into his surprised mouth and her body pressed him against a wall.

Frankie retained his virginity that evening, but the experience endowed him with a degree of sexual enlightenment that those magazines and his misinformed friends had not been able to accomplish. He saw the young woman on several other occasions and they shared additional intimacies without going all the way, which soon led her to seek a more experienced companion and taught him that romance is a transitory thing.

The end of the relationship was something of a relief to Frankie, whose other interests had to some extent been put aside while he attempted to entertain the young woman after school and in the evenings with little pocket money and even less experience at the enterprise. Once free again, he returned to those things he found interesting or entertaining, particularly the exploration on his bike of nearby parts of the city and particularly the great public park that had been laid out on its western perimeter.

The park was an enormous greensward and forest, providing natural relief from the concrete and asphalt so prevalent in the city, but it also offered a great deal more to anyone with sufficient time and curiosity to investigate its resources. There was a fine art museum on the crest of a broad hill that overlooked a man-made lagoon, where Frankie spent hours wandering its galleries with the particular purpose of viewing those paintings and sculptures that revealed naked female bodies. And while his original purpose had nothing to do with art, he inadvertently came to like what he saw. There came the gradual realization he was looking at pictures and statuary of fully clothed women and a wide variety of other things.

He was also drawn to the vast zoo with its many outside animal displays during the summer – everything from elephants and polar bears to a seemingly endless variety of antelopes – as well as a succession of buildings that separately housed primates, hippos, reptiles and other non-human animals that extended from the familiar to the exotic. At the time, children with bikes – even the older ones – were allowed onto the zoo grounds, where broad paved paths allowed them to safely peddle among the exhibits. Or they could chain their bikes to metal railings or the odd pole and leisurely inspect any of the infinite number of interesting things available to the relatively light crowds that milled about the place during the week. Frankie learned to avoid not only the zoo, but the entire park on summer weekends when great children-infested throngs assembled for picnics and other forms of amusement.

One of the park's principal attractions was a large, open air theater where something called "light opera" and musicals were performed to generally packed houses on sultry summer nights. In 1942, the Municipal Opera – where Frankie and several of his friends worked at entry-level jobs for pocket money – put on, among others, a production of "Desert Song" in which the lead character was a masked figure called "The Red Shadow." Based very roughly on the conflict between Berber tribesmen on the one hand and France and Spain on the other in the mid 1920s, the story was set in Morocco. The Red Shadow spent most of his time trying to induce the heroine into the desert, which he told her in almost uninterrupted song was about the most romantic place on earth. He neglected to explain, however, there was precious little water or anything else in the place. Like most of the others in the audience who sought escape from the depressing war news, Frankie bought the premise every night for the week the show ran.

In "Balilika," which was staged during a heat wave and set just before the 1917 revolution, one scene showed Russian soldiers at Christmas during the First World War. They wore heavy trench coats and one beat his arms against his chest to ward off the winter chill. "The cold gets in your bones," he said with quivering conviction, invoking peals of laughter from the sweat-soaked audience. The temperature was a steamy 90 degrees and the time was past 10 at night.

Frankie was an usher at the Municipal Opera,

showing patrons to their seats in the more expensive sections nearest a stage so broad and well lighted it was clearly visible to even those who sat in the most distant and elevated parts of the huge amphitheater. But for anyone who wanted to scrutinize the performers, there were concessions that rented small binoculars called "opera glasses" and provided employment for boys of Frankie's generation. Others in the same age group hawked cold beverages and ice cream during the long intermission at each performance.

Once those performances began, Frankie found a place off to the side where he could watch the shows, usually seated on some concrete step or leaning against a metal rail. As the weeks of the 1942 summer progressed, he got to know the guards who patrolled the backstage, and eventually gained occasional admittance to the area at the end of the evenings. He and a friend, Jack Smiley, were also allowed to stay for the midnight rehearsals conducted most Saturdays for the next production. A short, wiry boy with generally uncombed, red hair, Jack also worked at the Muny Opera and had been one of Frankie's schoolmates since kindergarten.

"Form a milling crowd," the director instructed the company in an authoritative baritone voice at one of the midnight rehearsals. The young singers and dancers wandered about for a few minutes before he stopped them with such displeasure his annoyance was clear to the sparse audience that sat in the comfortably cool early morning air that had settled on the park. "Goddammit," he shouted. "I said form a milling crowd. Every time I ask you goddamn people to form a goddamn crowd, you form a goddamn perfect circle."

"It may be a circle," Frankie said to Jack as they watched from two of the seats down front, "but it's not perfect."

The boys had met a veteran character actor, Leroy Miles, late in the season, and since they were going in the same direction cccasionally walked with him out of the park after the late rehearsals. As they crossed the broad, dark lawns and took short cuts over sections of the public golf course, he told them stories of stage and early motion picture actors in a rich professional voice that gave his material a ring of truth it probably didn't deserve. He told them he had been a guest and witness at William Randolph Hearst's California estate, San Simeon, in the 1920s when the wealthy press lord killed a man over the movie actress and Hearst mistress, Marion Davies. The victim's body was made to disapear and the few witnesses were made to understand there would be substantial consequences for anyone who disclosed the rich and powerful man's secret. "I might have been a motion picture star had I not been there," Miles said wistfully as they trod the dewy grass, although he failed to explain what the murder and his lost stardom had in common.

They usually walked while Miles talked until they emerged from the park, and he left them at the apartment hotel where he lodged during the theater season. The boys then walked on another five or more miles to their common neighborhood, where they parted and Frankie prepared himself for the predictable ritual that always accompanied his late arrival at home.

"Is that you, Frankie?" his mother would inquire as he tried to sneak past her bedroom through the hallway and only route to his room. The noisy front door inevitably awakened her from a light sleep.

"Yes, mom," he would reply and she would ask about the time. "It's a little after 10," he'd tell her, fully aware it was more than a little after three in the morning and that she couldn't read the clock next to her bed without glasses.

"Sleep well," she would then tell him and slip back into her dream world before he reached his room.

That summer separated Frankie from his childhood and the period of adolescence that led, awkwardly enough, to the adult world. He had graduated what was then called grammar school – which in those days ended with the eighth grade – and would begin high school in the early fall. And since most of his classmates would do the same, he assumed the confined, comfortable life he had known for the past years would continue with little change.

Frankie had been enrolled at the school in the first grade when he, six at the time, and his parents moved into the apartment he would occupy through the death of his father and most of his teenage years. His small back bedroom - had someone bothered to photograph its various stages – was a historical record of his growth and interests. As he aged, the juvenile toys were replaced by an old table with chemicals, flasks and test tubes he acquired individually from a neighborhood druggist for what he called his "laboratory," but was mainly used to make small, relatively harmless explosive devices. He and Jack Smiley, when they were about 10, made gunpowder, which they neatly folded into small squares of paper and put on streetcar tracks where the detonations made a good deal of noise but did no damage, if you ignored the occasional heart attack suffered by the occasional streetcar passenger.

The streetcars of Frankie's childhood were tall, yellow contrivances that swayed and rattled nosily, traversing the city day and night. In the years before the tracks were paved over and buses began to run on his street, the intermittent sound of passing trollies became such an integral part of his dream world that he found it difficult to sleep away from a noise that would keep the uninitiated awake. In summers when he was very young and his mother packed him off to visit his father's parents in a small, southern town, the insistent buzz of crickets at night rather than the rattle of streetcars kept him awake for a week before he acclimated to the strange difference.

Frankie's room and particularly the small desk next to a worn, four poster reflected his expanding occupations. He built model airplanes there with ultra-light balsa wood and, later, pecked out short articles on an old Underwood typewriter – given to him by his mother – for the neighborhood newspaper he produced with help from a supportive local printer who let him use an obsolete duplicating machine. Years later, he could still invoke the pungent smell of the glue used to construct those airplane models, inspired by such originals as the First World War Fokker Tri-plane and the P-40 flown by the Flying Tigers just before the Japanese attack on Pearl Harbor. A Fokker had been piloted by the German ace, Manfred von Richthofen, who shot down 80 enemy planes before he was killed in combat. And American volunteers flew the P-40s, which had tiger teeth boldly painted on the engine cowls, against the Japanese in China before U.S. entry into the war.

Frankie Bonner was an only child whose father died when he was 10 and whose mother worked long hours, but he was neither deprived of family nor affection. His mother's younger sister, Mary, was married to a steady man, Cleveland Coldstream, and they were the parents of four children, two boys and two girls, all younger than

Frankie. A gentle woman with a light touch, Aunt Mary treated Frankie like one of her own, and he had the run of her large but modest home within long walking distance of the apartment he shared with his mother. Her husband, too, was more of a surrogate father than an uncle, and the children were more like brothers and sisters than cousins. Frankie had access to a large, close family without the responsibilities. He could mingle with these noisy relatives when it suited him or seek the solitude of his own room when it didn't. "I lived in the best of all possible worlds," he thought years later when he recalled those times. In the summer of 1942, however, that revelation was still in the distant future.

*

Chapter Two

"Rats," Frankie Bonner thought to himself as he sat next to his nine-year-old cousin, Chester Coldstream, as the streetcar swayed wildly along at top speed on a rare stretch of open track. He had promised his Aunt Mary to take Chester, her youngest son, to the public swimming pool on a day his older brother and two sisters were otherwise occupied. He liked his little cousin well enough, but had been forced to take the streetcar rather than his bike because Mary thought public transportation was the safer alternative for the younger boy. Frankie preferred his bike because it enabled him to come and go on his own schedule rather than at the whim of some remote dispatcher for the transit authority.

The real summer – which includes those months before Labor Day and the beginning of the new school year – was fast fading, but the day was a splendid combination of blue almost cloudless sky, warm but not excessive temperatures and uncharacteristically low humidity for that time in the natural cycle. Neither of the boys, however, was particularly aware of these fortunate conditions or the pleasant breeze that swept across them from the open window next to their seats as they sat silently locked in their individual thoughts.

As far as Frankie was concerned, Chester was not the pest he could have been, but he had a habit that annoyed his older cousin. He liked to belch, not the result of any gastric disturbance but mostly for his own amusement and, perhaps, to garner attention from others. Frankie had originally instructed him on the grossness of his conduct, but gave up because Chester ignored him and the boy's mother took a tolerant attitude toward her son's gasiness. "Better to belch a belch and bear the shame than squelch a belch and bear the pain," Mary observed. Frankie knew there was no pain involved, only Chester's juvenile sense of humor, but he saw the futility of his protests and allowed the boy to belch his way through childhood.

Chester's volcanic belches were strangely absent so far that day because he was distracted by the panoramic nature of those things that appeared to him as the streetcar swept past such diverse tableaus as a pair of fornicating dogs and a fistfight between two young men in an alley. There were also the ordinary activities, a man mowing his grass and a woman hanging laundry on a clothesline, among others, but Chester watched patiently for the more offbeat stuff. He didn't really understand what the dogs were doing, but knew from experience it was something that often amused the adults.

Frankie's main concern was to get Chester to the pool, remain there long enough to satisfy his aunt and return the young relative home in time to salvage some part of the day. The pleasure he normally derived from swimming would be compromised by the need to watch

Chester, who had not yet learned to swim very well but had little apparent knowledge of that deficiency. He had the habit of plunging into deep water with little regard to whether or not he could make it back to where he began, and Frankie understood this problem better than his Aunt Mary. He knew he had to constantly watch Chester or run the risk of delivering the bad news to the boy's mother. "What a pain," he thought as the streetcar rattled along toward the suburban park where the large public pool had been constructed for anyone with the modest price of admission.

"Goin' swimming?" a rough and not particularly friendly voice inquired from a seat several rows behind them. Both Frankie and Chester had rolled their swimming trunks into towels, which was a convenient way to carry those items and an indication of their destination and purpose as well. Frankie was unaware three older boys had boarded the streetcar several stops back, and at first failed to realize the question from one of them was directed at him.

"Hey, stupid, are you deaf, too?" the voice asked as he began to understand the emerging problem. There were bullies or worse in the world and he had stumbled across at least one of them on a perfectly good summer day. "Oh, crap," he thought, aware the streetcar was approaching a stop within short walking distance of the swimming pool. He now wondered if he and Chester – who was completely unaware of the dilemma – could rid themselves of this nuisance when they got off the trolley. Chester, meanwhile, stared out the window, hopeful something as interesting as the coupled dogs would be revealed to his curious gaze.

"Are you dumb as well as deaf?" the voice persisted while Frankie tried to ignore it because he didn't know what to say. He had also come to realize his antagonist was not alone. He heard at least two other voices, although their tone was conversational and too low to be understood over the noisy rumble of the streetcar. Frankie's first impulse was to flee the problem at the next stop, confident his natural speed could probably get him away safely, but he then realized Chester's presence scratched that possibility. His scruffy young cousin could shoot marbles like a world champion, but would be no match for these older boys in a foot race. "Double crap," Frankie thought as he mentally rummaged for some other means of escape.

He had not yet learned there are seldom perfect solutions to the problems in life, which was the case that day. As a result, Frankie – devoid of a plan - fell back on pure instinct. As they approached the stop, he stood up, pulled the overhead cord that alerted the motorman he wanted to get off, and jerked Chester up and out of his hypnotic fascination with the outside world. Still unaware of their predicament, Chester followed him wordlessly past the center doors, which would slide open when they stopped, to the front of the streetcar. Frankie assumed there might be some advantage to making their exit past the motorman who, however, was barely aware of their presence. He had been delayed by traffic early on the run, and was more concerned with making up the lost time.

Once off the streetcar – which was on its way in a moment – Frankie saw with some trepidation that the three older boys had apparently followed him. They had left through the center doors and now stood half a streetcar length away, but too close for his personal comfort. Oddly, though, they didn't look as menacing as the one boy's voice had implied. They looked to Frankie like a matched set, all wearing relatively clean jeans and tee shirts and all about two years his senior. But any reassurance he might have derived from their appearance was soon dashed by another abrasive question from the tallest of the three who, it turned out, had the voice that taunted him earlier.

"You lookin' for trouble?" he shouted down the line. Frankie now realized there was no point in flight, and turned to confront the older boy who approached him in a casual, threatening manner. His friends followed a few steps behind while Chester watched the whole thing with complete detachment.

"No," Frankie replied, aware his response was not likely to satisfy someone whose only apparent purpose was to fight with him for no good reason.

"I heard what you said," the older boy partially explained, almost as if he'd read Frankie's mind. It was now obvious he either thought he'd been insulted or was simply lying as an excuse to cause trouble.

"I didn't say anything to you," Frankie said as his antagonist and the two others arrived within a few feet of where he stood with Chester, who attempted to support his cousin. "He didn't say anything to anybody," the nine-year-old chimed in.

"I'm not going to take that kind of crap from you or your midget friend," the older boy warned, although his companions didn't show any particular interest in the confrontation. "Let's go," one of them suggested, but the request fell on deaf ears. His aggressive friend was determined to see the matter through to some kind of conclusion. Frankie understood this reality but didn't know what to do about it. He was going to repeat his earlier denial when the older boy's fist struck him solidly on his right cheek and he dropped like a stone to the ground, momentarily stunned. "Get up and fight," the older boy demanded, confident his size and weight advantage would enable him to easily repeat what he had just done. Tall for his age, Frankie was only an inch or two shorter than his tormentor, but he lacked the 16-year-old's body strength. He had also never been in a fist fight and the solid punch he took came as a complete surprise. Somewhat confused, he lay on his back for a few moments before he struggled to his feet, only to meet another punch to the other cheek that put him, once again, flat on his back.

"You jerk," Chester said to the older boy, who ignored him.

The second punch had also caught Frankie squarely, forcing a tooth through his cheek but he would not realize any discomfort from the wound until later. At the moment, he felt a tide of rising anger, partially because he now hated the unfairness of his predicament and partly because he was embarrassed to take a beating in Chester's presence. He was supposed to be his young cousin's protector and it now appeared he couldn't protect himself.

"Damn," he thought and got up again, nearly catching a third punch that missed his head by inches. This time, he rushed the larger boy in an effort to fight back, but only caught another blow that bloodied his nose and put him, again, on his back.

"That's enough," one of the older boy's friends said. He had not realized until then that Frankie was, by teenage standards, a good deal younger than he had originally thought. "He's just a kid."

"He's a smart ass kid," the older boy remarked, his anger subsiding somewhat as he stared at Frankie's bloody face and dusty clothes. He failed to notice, however, that Frankie, as he lay on the ground, had inadvertently found a rock that fit perfectly into his right hand. He also thought the fight was over and failed to react when the fallen kid rose with unexpected energy and hit him squarely in the face with that rock, breaking his nose and sending him, unconscious, to the ground for a change. Unlike Frankie, he lay there face down with his arms out to the sides like a bird poised for flight.

"Jesus," one of the older boy's friends said, staring at his body and not knowing for several moments whether he was dead or alive. Shortly, however, a moan, muffled because he lay face down in a patch of dirt, revealed the blow he had taken was not fatal. Frankie, battered and breathing heavily, dropped the rock and recovered his towel and swim suit, which had gone flying across a nearby patch of grass when the fight began.

"Beat it," the older boy's other friend instructed Frankie, aware there would be further trouble if he remained long enough for his injured companion to regain consciousness. Frankie, too, understood that probability and motioned Chester to join him as he crossed the tracks to catch a homeward bound streetcar which approached at that particular moment in a stroke of blind luck. As the injured boy rolled onto his back, groaning and still dazed, Chester leaned over him and issued a prolonged belch before he trotted off to join his cousin and board the approaching trolley. "Jerk," he said, mostly to himself.

Chester understood there would be no swimming that day, although he didn't bother to consider the reasons, which mostly included Frankie's battered condition and the need to avoid an area where the older boy might find them. "I don't care that much about swimming, anyway," Chester explained later when Frankie told him they'd do it some other day. "I'd rather shoot marbles."

At nine, Chester was a marble shark, a child wizard among children who bet marbles on their skill at the game. If marbles had been money, Chester – who had won thousands of these little glass and agate balls, mostly from unsuspecting juveniles – would have been the wealthiest kid in town. His version of the game was called "ringer," in which a circle is drawn in the dirt and the players take turns knocking other players' marbles out of the circle with their own marble. Although Chester gave no thought to the history of his sport, marbles were mentioned in Roman literature and there are many examples from ancient Egypt.

Drawn to the game by discovery of his own natural talent, Chester was as much a brilliant con artist as he was a premature athlete. A skinny boy, usually with his shirt tail half out, he knew how to sucker those who didn't know him into a game, particularly those who were bigger and stronger and who usually thought he was unlikely to present much of a challenge. He was also smart enough not to gloat when he won, which made him something of a popular champion among those familiar with his rather specialized abilities. Most of his young friends called him Chet, but he was Chester to everyone in his family.

Their mothers were sisters, but Frankie and Chester bore no physical resemblance to one another. Frankie's straight, dark brown hair looked combed, even when it wasn't, and Chester's hair, much lighter, never appeared combed, even when it was. The younger boy's appearance was unruly, but his disposition was restrained, even thoughtful.

"Don't tell your mother about the fight," Frankie told Chester as they rode home on the streetcar, aware by then of the aches and soreness that had been inflicted on him. He felt as though his whole head was a unified bruise and that his face had probably turned dark blue as a result. Actually, he had gotten off rather well in that regard. The spot where the tooth pierced his jaw, although subject to infection, was minute, and his other injuries only amounted to a few facial scrapes that he later attributed for his mother's sake to a minor accident.

"Okay," Chester agreed without questioning the need for an occasional lie to one's parents. These untruths protected what little freedom there was in childhood, and had nothing to do with any obligation a kid might have to a mother or father.

Frankie had been embarrassed by the beating he took, but Chester saw the bigger picture. "You sure gave that jerk what he needed," he said. "I'll bet he saw stars when you nailed him with that rock."

The fight had been something of an epiphany for Frankie, who had rough-housed with his friends but had never before been in a contest where someone really meant to hurt him. He had seen fights in the movies and in the school yard, but he was a good natured boy who had escaped real violence through most of his young life. But he learned that day there were unreasonable people and circumstances in the world capable of changing things for the worse on a moment's notice. And he wondered how many times the older boy would have knocked him down had he not found that rock and the strength to use it. As he and Chester rode home on the streetcar, these thoughts assembled in his mind and slowly led to a conclusion. The best way to avoid beatings of the kind he just took was to learn how to fight, he reasoned. Meanwhile, Chester had rediscovered the world that raced past the window next to him. There were no copulating dogs this time, but he did notice a large cat perched high up in a tree, barely visible through the heavy foliage, and a small group of boys rummaging through a pile of trash someone had deposited in an alley. These momentary tableaus would have gone unnoticed by most people, but seemed to interest Chester, whose absorption was apparent in his failure to belch, even once.

Frankie took Chester to a White Castle and bought him cheap hamburgers and a carbonated drink with money originally intended to pay their way into the swimming pool. He did it partly to compensate his cousin for the lost day and partly to kill time before taking the boy home. He knew his Aunt Mary's suspicions would surely be aroused if they returned too soon. As it turned out, she was gone – as were Chester's older brother and two sisters – when they arrived at the old, two story, gray brick house which, as usual, was unlocked with a number of the windows open to the pleasant late summer breeze. Her absence proved a break for Frankie, who had forgotten his battered appearance as he acclimated to the pain in his jaws and cheeks that would remain with him for several days. He took advantage of the situation to carefully wash the blood and dirt from his face and dust his clothes off as best he could.

"Will you be okay alone?" he asked Chester as he left the house.

"Why not?" Chester said and belched, unintentionally for a change. He had eaten more than his share of sliders because Frankie's jaws were in no condition to chew much of anything.

"And don't say anything about the fight," Frankie

reminded the boy as he descended the steps off the front stoop, his towel and trunks tucked under one arm and the pain in his face deflecting other sensations from the rest of his body.

“Okay,” Chester replied, recollection of the fight fading from his thoughts even as he closed the front door and went about his juvenile business.

“What happened to you?” Nicolas Satterfield ask Frankie the next day.

“I had an accident,” Frankie explained, repeating the same explanation he had used with his mother that very morning.

Nick Satterfield looked at him in a way that told the boy he might fool his mother with that story, but not him. “I’d guess you ran into a fist,” he said.

Frankie, who saw Nick as an old man despite his compact muscularity and considerable energy at 50, liked his mother’s boyfriend, and wasn’t really surprised that his little fib had not worked with him. Nick seemed to know things that others didn’t.

“You won’t tell my mom?” Frankie asked with some confidence it wasn’t going to be a problem.

“Not likely, but I still want to know what happened,” Nick said. He had developed an almost paternal attitude toward the boy during the past year in which his attachment to the mother had gone from casual to borderline monogamous. He had known many women intimately over the years but had never married, mainly because he had usually not been in one place long enough to establish permanent relationships.

“I got the piss beat out of me,” Frankie confessed, and then told Nick the complete story, including the part where he laid the older boy low with a rock. “I’m not much of a fighter,” he added with the objectivity that was part of his nature.

"Probably not," Nick agreed, "but you did what you had to do, and there's something to be said for that." He gave the matter additional consideration, and then said: "Do you want to learn to fight?"

"Yes," the boy replied, thinking of Joe Louis and the beating he had inflicted on Buddy Baer earlier that year. He made some reference to the match to show his enthusiasm for the project.

"I said fight, not box," Nick said. "There's an important difference you need to understand if we're going to do this thing." He went on to explain he meant bare-knuckled, hand-to-hand combat that had nothing to do with Marquis of Queensberry rules.

"What's the Marquis of Queensberry?"

"Look it up," Nick instructed, and told him to forget Joe Louis and Buddy Baer. "You were closer to what I have in mind when you picked up that rock and saved your bacon." Nick told Frankie his program would start with strength training in a nearby YMCA weight room and, later, when he was stronger, with fight instruction he would personally provide. He didn't tell him the instruction was related to martial arts training he had received many years earlier in the Far East. But he did tell him he didn't want his time wasted, and would only help if he swore to see it through to the end. "Think about it before you make a commitment," Nick advised. Frankie agreed, although he knew at the time he would accept the offer. The beating he received taught him there were nasty people around, and he was determined never again to be one of their victims.

Frankie instinctively trusted Nick to deliver on the training he promised, although he knew next to nothing about the man's credentials in that regard. He didn't know that his mother's lover had traveled the world as a young man and had seen service with both the French Foreign Legion and the U.S. Marine Corps in the First World War. Frankie, in fact, had never heard of the Foreign Legion, although he had some knowledge of the war as the result of the many veterans of the conflict – neighbors and local tradesmen among them – he knew and whose occasional stories gave that great event immediacy for him. Frankie knew vaguely about the Battle of the Somme in 1916, one of the bloodiest military operations in history. Fought before American entry into the war, there were a million and a half English, French and German casualties. The British alone suffered well over 57,000 casualties, including more than 19,000 dead on July 1st when the battle began.

Frankie knew a little more about Belleau Wood in northern France where the Marines suffered substantial losses but were instrumental in halting the final German offensive late in the war. But he didn't know that Nick Satterfield, only in his 20s at the time, had fought in both battles.

In France a year before the war broke out, Nick enlisted in the Foreign Legion on nothing more than a whim and to break the monotony of the merchant marine service that had kept him at sea for long periods of time as he sought ever newer places and experiences. An elite unit with the French army, the Legion – made up mostly of foreign volunteers – was established in 1831 to protect and expand the nation's colonial empire.

Nick survived the Battle of the Somme and others on the Western Front mostly through sheer luck that might have run out late in the war when the Legion suffered particularly heavy casualties. Instead, he and others from various countries were released to serve in their national armies, which gave him an opportunity to narrowly escape death in a Marine Corps uniform at Belleau Wood. Smart enough to know he'd cheated the odds, he returned to the United States after the war with the sure knowledge he would never again put on a military uniform.

Nick had left home and high school in his junior year when he beat his alcoholic father – who had beaten him for years – into unconsciousness. His mother had died somewhat earlier and he left with no regrets, even though it occurred to him that the parent he last saw stretched out on their front room floor might well be dead. He had hit him squarely in the head with a baseball bat.

He then rode the rails from his Nebraska home to New Orleans – sustaining himself along the way with odd jobs and petty theft – and hung out in a maritime union hall long enough to get the papers he needed to ship out on a rusted old vessel that made its way to and through the Panama Canal onto the broad Pacific and eventually a succession of exotic oriental ports. Nick began in the ship's engine room as a wiper and worked his way up to more skilled positions until – jaded after several years with the sights and scents of both eastern and western ports and tired of the long passages – he jumped ship in France and soon found himself in the middle of a general war he had not foreseen.

Nick never discussed the First War or anything else about his background with Frankie or his mother, and made only vague references to the line of work that made him appear prosperous, if not actually wealthy. He dressed well – usually in a conservative suit and tie – and drove a late model black Buick that was never low on gasoline through all the long years of home front rationing. Nick, in fact, seemed to have ready access to the many goods that were in short supply during the Second World War.

"Where do you get this stuff?" Frankie's mother asked him one evening when he gave her an attractively wrapped package that contained six pairs of nylon stockings, something that had disappeared from store shelves when the material was allocated for production of military parachutes.

"One of my clients owed me a favor," he explained, which was sufficient to satisfy her curiosity and of no concern to Frankie, who heard virtually the same explanation when Nick produced other things that were not generally available at the time. Nick's occasional allusion to clients who had access to everything from Hershey bars to automobile tires – all as difficult to find as nylons – was remotely suspicious but his appearance and manner provided, at least for Frankie and his mother, an aura of respectability. That aura was entirely misleading since Nick Satterfield was a small time but reasonably successful criminal.

Nick returned from the war with little in the way of skills other than those he had acquired in ship engine rooms and on a succession of bloody battlefields. There were millions of others who had survived the war, but relatively few who had endured such sustained carnage without suffering at least minor psychological damage. Not Nick, however, who emerged from the death and rat-ridden trenches of France with essentially the same level disposition and outlook with which he had entered an unexpected war.

Back in the United States, he had only been able to find menial, boring work at low pay until he received a phone call from Tim O'Malley, who had served with him at Belleau Wood. A recipient of the Purple Heart, Tim had been shot in the ass with a stray bullet that probably came from friendly fire. In any event, the injury was neither intentional nor serious since it hit him in a fleshy region of his large backside and did no permanent damage.

"There's a job open with my Uncle Tom and I told him about you," Tim explained in a long distance call Nick knew was expensive. He was also a bit surprised because he and Tim had been friendly, but not all that close. He also wondered how Tim, who lived in Chicago, had tracked him to the run-down boarding house in St. Louis, where he lived at the time.

"What kind of job?" he asked. The answer he received was vague except for the salary information, which was a good deal more than anything he had managed to earn since his return from France. But Tim, he recalled, often got him into trouble of various kinds, mostly because he drank heavily and was a mean drunk who liked nothing better than to start fights with anyone and their friends. As a result, his mouth was populated by only about half the teeth nature had given him, and his nose was a good deal flatter than it might have been.

One night during the war and in a small bistro full of battle-weary French soldiers, Nick recalled that Tim, drunker even than usual, had suddenly stood up at the table where they had sat for several hours and hurled a wine bottle at the large mirror behind the bar. "I hate you fucking French bastards," he screamed as the mirror broke and fell in shards to the floor. "And I hate your beat-up, God-damned country," he added while several English-speaking Frenchmen translated his words for the others and Nick sneaked quietly but rapidly out of the place.

Later, Tim – who had miraculously survived the night but had been badly beaten by a small mob of outraged allies – regained consciousness and some degree of sobriety in a cobblestone gutter outside the bistro, where Nick found and dragged him to his feet. “Thanks, old buddy,” Tim mumbled, under the impression Tim had fought side by side with him. That mistaken gratitude, Nick assumed, had something to do with the phone call and job offer.

Nick was absolutely right in that assumption. Tim had told his uncle that Nick was “a hard-nosed, stand-up guy” who would be useful to “the business.” The business, as Nick discovered later, was a small-time criminal enterprise that was on the brink of expansion as the result of Prohibition, which began in 1920 and banned the sale, manufacture and transportation of liquor throughout the United States. With no other prospects he could discern, Nick took the job and moved to Chicago where he soon learned he was expected to do things that were not only illegal but dangerous as well. He had small objection to the illegalities, but he had seen enough danger in his life that far to seek safer alternatives. Uncle Tom had originally intended to use him for muscle in the tough neighborhoods where he ran his rackets, but Nick persuaded him that unspecified “battlefield injuries” had rendered him ill-equipped for that work. And while the old, cigar-chomping crook probably didn't buy the story, he realized that Nick was both smart and glib – qualities that were in short supply in his organization – and found other, less physically demanding things for him to do.

He eventually became something of a surrogate nephew to Uncle Tom after the real one, Tim, got himself beaten to death in a local episode that resembled the one in the French bistro. Nick was a slick operator compared to Uncle Tom, whose rough edges antagonized his underworld competitors and eventually got him killed when the local gangs began to seriously compete for the lucrative trade in illegal liquor and beer. Luckily for him, Nick was able to elude a couple of thugs bent on sending him to wherever Uncle Tom went, and he clandestinely returned to St. Louis where he established over the years a base for a wide variety of illegal schemes that were not competitive with any of the established criminal organizations. Essentially a gentleman, Nick refused to defraud women and children, particularly widows and orphans. However, he considered almost anyone else fair game.

Nick's reluctance to fight had everything to do with his recollection of the corpse-strewn French battlefields and nothing to do with his abilities, which would have been sufficient to handle the muscle stuff for Uncle Tom had he wanted that work. He was much stronger than he appeared, and his natural quickness and large hands gave him a fighting edge he seldom employed, preferring to talk rather than fight his way out of controversies. He was not a pacifist, though, only a realist who understood from experience that physical violence was best left as a last resort. He wanted to provide Frankie – who he had come to regard as a son – with this knowledge as well as the ability to defend himself when there were no better alternatives.

Nick's martial arts training – fragmented and limited by the shortness of his tenure in a variety of Asian countries during his sea-faring days – made him a tougher fighter, but he never fully understood the discipline he pursued was meant to shape his mind and spirit as well as his body. He was a practical rather than a spiritual man, and a life time of training would probably have done little to change him. But he did instill in Frankie his own belief that violence was best left as a last resort, and he did it with selective reminders over the next few years as the boy proved a talented student with relentless intensity that would one day provide him with capacities far beyond those of his teacher.

*

Chapter Three

In 1944, many of Frank Bonner's 16 or 17-year-old friends carried a condom in their wallets, but were still several years away from anything that would resemble a complete sexual experience. Most of these condoms – commonly called "rubbers" – would remain unused, eventually embossing a small but perfect circle on a slew of leather billfolds where the devices gradually dried out to the point of near disintegration.

Frank, too, carried an obligatory condom, but knew it was unlikely to find use because his girl friend, Molly Bacon, was too prudent to risk pregnancy with something that wasn't a guaranteed safeguard. In the long years before modern contraceptive measures were developed, the prospect and fear of accidental motherhood was a reasonably but not entirely effective form of protection. Since the girls in those days had more to lose than their boyfriends, they were the first line of restraint. But these young women had hormones, too, which meant there was between couples a good deal of kissing, groping and rubbing together that was a principal means of sexual expression.

"I love you, Molly," Frank said as he clumsily

unlatched the bra strap under the soft, powder blue sweater that matched her eyes. They sat on the steps in the vestibule of the apartment building where she lived with her mother and sister and where they had been kissing each other for some time.

"Me, too," she said, meaning she felt the same way about him but saying something quite different. Their modified love making had over time been ritualized, although its repetition in no way reduced the intensity of their feelings. She had slapped him ever so gently the first time he tried to fondle her breasts, but the restraint she showed told him it was okay. From then on, they had gone a little further each week following their Saturday night dates, always stopping short of the ultimate act. Their reluctance to go beyond a certain point, however, was usually the result of location as much as it was the fear of an unintended pregnancy. The apartment building vestibule was generally unoccupied at that time of night, but it was entirely too public a place for anything that couldn't be quickly disguised should anyone arrive or leave the place.

"What's that," she said nervously as he elevated the bottom of her sweater to reveal small but well formed breasts that had been liberated from the unsnapped brassiere. They sat on the steps below the second floor landing, a calculated position that afforded as much privacy as possible in an essentially public space.

"Just the wind against the front door," he said, not entirely sure he was right but anxious to provide her with reassurance. She listened for a moment to confirm that reassurance, and then settled her head against his shoulder as he kissed one of her nipples. Her body had a pleasant floral aroma he assumed was natural, unaware the scent had originated in a cologne bottle.

"Are you and Jack thinking about enlisting in the Army?" she asked, partly because the question was serious and partly to distract from the reality of his hand, which was now lifting the hem of her skirt. They had met Frank's friend, Jack Smiley, earlier that evening at The Park Bench, a high school hang-out where they had gone for something to eat following the Saturday night movie.

"The Marine Corps, not the Army," he replied. Frank went on to explain they were at 16 still too young to enlist, but could do it with a parent's consent at 17. He didn't tell her, though, that he thought the war would be over by the time he was old enough to serve or that his stepfather, Nick Satterfield, who had married his mother more than a year earlier, would have done his best to persuade him otherwise. Nick, he knew, would also try to persuade his mother not to grant her permission. Frank still didn't know that Nick's antipathy to war – even a just war – was based on the carnage he had witnessed at the Battle of the Marne and Belleau Wood, among other bloody places. Quietly glib about most things, Nick had never discussed the First War or his part in it with his new family.

"I'd rather be here with you than in the Marine Corps," Frank whispered to Molly following a long, deep kiss that coincided with the track of his hand up her slender, bare leg.

"Swell," she said quietly, "you like me better than war."

"Somewhat," he admitted as she removed her own underpants to preserve that delicate article from his eager teenage grasp. This, too, was part of the established ritual, which they combined with passionate expectations and casual conversation.

"Do you really want to get involved in that awful war?"

Molly inquired, mainly to cover her rising passion in a verbal way because the physical experience was still relatively new and somewhat embarrassing for her. Frank, too, was a novice at these intimacies, but they were both discovering that repetition gradually made the whole effort seem more natural.

"Not really," he said, barely aware his answer was a complete lie. He and Jack wanted to go to war because they thought it would be a great adventure. They had no notion of the mortal consequences the current conflict had extracted from millions of others. But he now followed current events closely and knew a good deal about the progress of the war, both because he was curious by nature and hopeful it would last until he was old enough to take part in what was an extraordinary historical event.

Frank's suspicion the war wouldn't last until he was old enough to join the Marine Corps was supported by a substantial gathering of Allied military achievements around the world in 1944. Just after midnight on June sixth, the largest invasion force in history assaulted the German army on the French coast in Normandy at a series of beaches between Cherbourg and LeHavre. The Allies under the supreme command of General Dwight Eisenhower employed some 4000 landing craft, 700 ships, 10,000 planes, 176,000 troops and by the end of the first day, despite heavy casualties, more than 150,000 of those troops were dug in on that invasion coast along with thousands of vehicles and many tons of material. Although there would be delays and setbacks in the coming months, the D-Day landing was the beginning of an inexorable move eastward that would culminate less than a year later in the German surrender.

In the fall of the same year, U.S. forces under command of General Douglas MacArthur returned to the Philippines, invading at Leyte Island. MacArthur – who had promised to return when he escaped the conquering Japanese in 1942 – disembarked a ship and waded ashore to dramatize that return, which led the comedian, Mort Saul, to observe that the imperious general would have walked on the water but the U.S. president wouldn't let him.

In an attempt to disrupt the invasion, the Japanese sent a major naval force into Leyte Gulf, where it was met and defeated by the American navy. The loss by the Japanese in this engagement of 24 large ships, including four aircraft carriers, three battleships and 10 cruisers reduced a once formidable naval power to reliance on Kamikaze or aerial suicide attacks as they were pushed back in bloody island by island struggles toward their own island homeland.

Somewhat earlier, a French general and his forces reclaimed Paris from the Germans who had occupied it since 1940, and still later the U.S. Army entered Germany for the first time, although bitter fighting still lay ahead before the European war would end. But the handwriting was clearly on the wall in 1944 – writ large in German and Japanese – as American bombers reached southern Japan, Britain's Eighth Army liberated Florence in Italy, and the Russians captured 100,000 German soldiers at Minsk. These events left Frank Bonner with a patriotic and personal dilemma. He was stirred and proud of the military achievements of his country and its allies, but depressed by the notion it would all end before he could join in the effort.

"Call me tomorrow," she whispered from her apartment doorway as he descended the short bank of stairs to the vestibule where he had left a pair of sneakers for the run home. As usual, he had missed the last streetcar for the night – which ran along Union Avenue several blocks away – but was accustomed to covering the six miles on foot that separated his apartment building from hers. In fact, he preferred the long run in the cool darkness to the boring wait for the streetcars, which ran at uncertain intervals in the few hours before the service shut down for the night. He could run on his own schedule and his thoughts came to him with particular clarity as he jogged through the deserted streets, the laces to his street shoes tied together and slung over his shoulder.

His first recollections were usually of Molly and the intimacies they had just shared, but the sheer physicality of the run inevitably pounded sex from his thoughts and made room for other matters. Frank had just declined an invitation from Molly to attend church with her the next day, using as an excuse his occasional job at a small airport across the Mississippi River in Illinois where he worked most Sundays and some Saturdays for flying instruction. The excuse was reasonably valid, but he didn't tell her he found churches more boring than the long wait for a streetcar late at night. And he liked her too much to risk an admission he had serious doubts about certain fundamental religious postulations.

"I don't buy this stuff about a parted Red Sea any more than I think Christ or anyone else rose from the dead," he had told Jack Smiley a week earlier, dismissing the old and new testaments in a single effort. "And why in hell would anyone name their kid Moses?' he added as an afterthought.

"You're probably going to hell," Jack had replied before they changed the subject to more immediate considerations.

As he ran through the night on his way home, Frank recalled a favorable weather forecast for the next day, which meant there would be work for him at the airport. He had a weekday job after school that paid wages and provided money to support his teenage needs, but his work at the small, remote air field was done entirely for flying instructions. He had not yet soloed, but was approaching the point where he would soon pilot the Piper J-3 Cub on his own, and the prospect fully occupied his thoughts during the final minutes before his arrival at the apartment building that had been his home since early boyhood. He could visualize the plane's Spartan instrument panel with fewer than a half dozen gauges, and almost feel the thrust generated at full throttle by its modest 65 horsepower Continental engine. Once aloft, the small, yellow aircraft cruised at about 75 miles an hour and had a service ceiling of 11,500 feet, although it took a patient pilot with plenty of time to nudge the plane to that altitude. But the Midwestern skies in 1944 were uncluttered with commercial air traffic, and Frank felt a sense of release when he took the joystick from his instructor and flew out over the flat Illinois landscape with its rigid section lines broken only by the curved lake just west of the airport and the broad Mississippi River even further beyond.

"Incredible," Frank said aloud even though there was no one else in the hangar full of small aircraft parked in ways that accommodated the irregular shapes to one another. He had been waxing one of his instructor's Cubs – carefully applying and removing the paste on its various fabric surfaces – when he took a short break and discovered a name stenciled on the door of a nearby aircraft. "Douglas Corrigan," he read to himself, instantly aware the plane had probably been owned at one time by the man who famously flew the Atlantic in 1938 from the U.S. to Ireland without government permission.

Nicknamed "Wrong Way" Corrigan for a flight he blamed on cloud cover and a navigational error, everyone – even the 10-year-old Frankie Bonner – knew the pilot had simply ignored the bureaucrats who refused to let him fly a make-shift, patched-up pile of junk on a long and dangerous trip over ocean waters. Frank was contemplating the over-sized, two passenger plane when Bill Hager, his instructor and boss at the airport, came into the hangar. "What's up?" he inquired out of habit rather than curiosity. Frank answered the question with one of his own. "Have you seen this?" he asked, indicating Corrigan's name on the aircraft door.

"Sure," Hager replied, "but nobody around here knows for sure if Corrigan ever owned the damned thing or if someone else just put his name on it."

"I like to think it was his," Frank said, admiring the big metal propeller, unlike the much smaller wooden ones on all the other planes in the hangar. "He's got to be one brave son-of-a-gun."

"I'll give him that," Hager allowed, "but I also think he's one crazy son-of-a-bitch." He thought for a moment and then modified his assessment. "Actually," he continued, "the man's a first rate mechanic and a good pilot who's inclined to put his ass on the line when some hare-brained stunt strikes his fancy." He went on to explain that Corrigan worked for the company that built Charles Lindbergh's "Spirit of St. Louis" and was responsible for installation of the wing assembly, gas tanks and instrument panel on the plane that in 1927 carried its previously obscure pilot to instant

International and eventual long-term celebrity.

Hager also explained that Corrigan had flown his plane from Floyd Bennett Field in Brooklyn to Casement Aerodrome, County Dublin with the cockpit floor awash in gasoline leaking from an unrepaired fuel tank he had simply ignored to maintain his schedule. The flight took more than 28 hours and Corrigan's provisions amounted to a couple of chocolate bars, two boxes of fig bars and a quart of water. "The breakfast of champions," Hager observed.

Hager could have added but didn't that Corrigan's plane had fuel tanks mounted on the front that only allowed him to see out of the sides, and that he had no radio and a 20-year-old compass. The nose of the engine hood was a patchwork soldered together by the pilot himself and the door behind which he crouched during the long flight was fastened together with pieces of baling wire. And the reserve gas tanks he installed left him so little room that he flew the trip hunched forward with his knees cramped and not enough space to see the ground when he landed.

"What did they do to him?" Frank asked, meaning what kind of punishment was doled out to someone who broke every flying rule in the book.

"Not much," Hager said. "His pilot's certificate was suspended for two weeks." Aviation officials, however, took 600 words to list the regulations broken by his flight and they did it in a telegram at a time when the expense was calculated by the word.

"You about done with my plane," Hager said at last, an indication he had exhausted the subject of Douglas Corrigan. He looked around the hangar to assure himself everything was in order, and then hobbled away toward his make-shift office in a small nearby building on legs that had been mangled some years back in a plane crash that nearly took his life. The accident and a long recovery – coupled with hard drinking and faint attention to his general health – had taken its toll on the man. At 52, his weathered face and thin, gray hair made him look 20 years older. And the arthritis that had settled into his formerly broken bones made him feel at least that old, particularly when the weather was cold and damp.

"I'll be finished in half an hour," Frank called after him and returned to work. He didn't know much about Bill Hager, other than the general comments he had heard from others around the airport. They said he had been an Army pilot in the First World War and seen service in France where he had been twice shot down by the same German ace. Ironically, Hager had survived both crashes and the war while the man who knocked him out of the skies did not. Later, Hager had flown the U.S. mail in the early days of that service and still later barn-stormed around the mid-west like some aerial gypsy until the final crash that influenced his decision to seek a more settled life.

Hager – who had often slept in a blanket roll under the wing of his old bi-plane in his barnstorming days – had accumulated more savings than anyone who knew him suspected from a man of his casual nature and appearance. He used those funds to buy half interest in the airport where he now presided over several aircraft used for everything from flight instruction and rentals to the transport of anything to anywhere within reasonable distance.

Frank, who had finished work on the plane and now sought something else to do, was within a few feet of the door to Hager's office when he realized something out of the ordinary was going on. There was a loud, angry voice, unintelligible until he entered the building and was able to distinguish a torrent of profanity from a man who had pinned Hager against a wall and held him there with a single hand pressed hard against his throat. His other hand was a clenched fist, which he waved about wildly. “You miserable old goat,” he screamed, “you either give me my money or I’ll beat the living crap out of you.”

“Kiss my ass,” Hager gasp, his face red from the struggle and his arms limp at his sides.

“Put him down,” Frank said instinctively in a stern voice he barely recognized as his own. “Put him down, I say.”

The man – somewhere in his late 30s and dressed in grease-stained brown coveralls – glanced momentarily in Frank’s direction but kept his grip on Hager’s throat. “Mind your own business, kid, or you’ll get what I’ve got in store for this old bastard.” He cocked his fist and would have delivered a punch had Frank not grabbed him around the neck from behind and simultaneously planted his foot on the man’s calf, which dropped him down on a knee where he struggled to get up just as the young man’s fist hit him squarely on a cheek and he fell back on the floor. Hager, too, sank to the floor and sat there propped against the wall.

“Are you okay?” Frank asked Hager while the other man sat up and considered his options. He promptly decided Frank was more formidable than he’d originally thought. “I’ll settle with you later,” he mumbled as he regained his footing and crossed the room unsteadily to the door, which he slammed behind him and left with his anger still unresolved.

“I’m just dandy,” Hager replied, still seated on the floor and not looking all that good. “That bone-headed moron thinks he's a mechanic, but he couldn't fix a flat tire with God's help." He only bothered to explain that much because Frank had spared him a beating, although he had been battered and bruised so many times in his knock-about life that another trauma wouldn't have made that much difference. "You handled that guy pretty good," he said after a while and never mentioned the matter again. He was surprised, however, at Frank's apparent strength and ability to handle himself in a fight, even though the man he had just bested was something less than a robust specimen. The mechanic was, in fact, a skinny weakling and would have had trouble with almost anyone other than the depleted Bill Hager.

But Frank Bonner at 16 was a good deal stronger than Hager suspected, and had restrained the angry mechanic with only the minimum force needed to prevent him from pummeling the older man. He had developed the capacity by then to do real damage in a fight with most men, something he had learned from Nick Satterfield and a trainer, Fletcher Woo, who was remotely Chinese but had spent years in various Far Eastern countries before he illegally emigrated to the United States before the recent war broke out. He had been clandestinely brought into the country by a criminal boss to handle specialized assignments that required non-lethal but substantial physical violence. The two men, Satterfield and Woo, had met in Chicago, where they became friendly mainly because Woo's local associates at the time were almost exclusively big city gangsters and Satterfield was the rare exception who knew something about Asian cultures as the result of his maritime travels. Their friendship was cemented a few years later when Nick gave Fletcher a sanctuary in St.

Louis from a murder contract put out on him in Chicago as the result of complicated circumstances they never discussed. Woo laid low until he assumed the underworld had lost interest in him, working in a series of Chinese restaurants until he opened one of his own with Nick's financial backing and became a moderately successful businessman in his own right. Given his history with Nick, he was more than willing to take Frankie Bonner on as something of a student and turn him into the Frank Bonner who had plucked the unlucky assailant off Bill Hager.

Hager neither knew about any of this nor would have cared, but he did appreciate in his own disgruntled way Frank's pluck in confronting the outraged, unpaid and unworthy mechanic who had done expensive damage to an aircraft engine he was supposed to overhaul. Hager showed his appreciation over the next year with more weekend flight instruction and access to his planes than Frank could have earned working full time.

"I don't know what you see in that God-forsaken cow pasture," Jack Smiley said to Frank in reference to the airport on the Monday after his friend's confrontation with the mechanic. They were on their break in the alley behind Woo's Oriental Palace, where they both worked as part-time waiters several evenings a week. Jack had once gone to the airport with Frank, but had been put off by the multiple bus rides – one across the broad Mississippi River – and the need to hitchhike the last three miles down a near deserted Illinois state road to get there from their homes in the west end of St. Louis on the Missouri side. He had also gotten air sick on the single, short flight he took as a passenger in a small plane on a particularly turbulent afternoon. "I'd just as soon go to the frickin' moon," Jack added, recalling the partially-digested lunch he'd thrown up on the dark green grass immediately after the plane landed.

"You just hit a patch of rough air, and ought to give it another try," Frank said with indifferent sympathy. He did not tell him that flight instruction was part of a personal master plan that was still a work in progress. He figured the ability to pilot a plane coupled with a variety of other skills would prepare him for something he had not yet fully defined. He also liked to fly for its own sake, but that particular feeling would have been hard for him to express and he preferred to keep things like that to himself.

"You're strange," Jack observed because he was not likely to disclose the admiration he felt for his friend's accomplishments. He had watched Frank build himself into one of the strongest boys at their high school, using the school's weight room and other facilities but declining several invitations from coaches to join various athletic teams. He knew Frank trained in the martial arts, but didn't know their employer at the restaurant, Fletcher Woo, was the trainer just as he didn't know Nick Satterfield had set him on that path two years earlier.

Frank had come to respect Fletcher Woo, not only for his martial arts instruction, but also for the combination of strength and reserve that were fundamental to his nature. Over time, Woo, too, developed an unexpressed fondness for his student that forged a relationship between them that was not unlike an uncle and his favorite nephew.

Frank knew nothing of his instructor's hard background and had no notion the quiet restaurant owner had at one time beaten dozens of men senseless and inadvertently killed a few for his criminal employer. He also didn't know that Woo – not out of regret but because he felt underpaid for his work and disrespected for his race – had quit the crime organization that had employed him and sought a more profitable connection. He had anticipated the contract that was put out on his life, but his substantial pride and an essential fearlessness had over-ridden any other considerations. As it developed, he simply left Chicago and resettled in St. Louis with Nick Satterfield's help, and in time figured the mob had lost interest in his defection.

Jack Smiley was mostly puzzled by his friend's application to so many things for reasons that weren't readily apparent. Frank trained as a swimmer without any inclination to join the school swim team, and he grounded himself in subjects as disparate as outdoor survival and ancient history for equally opaque motives. He didn't know that Frank was driven by a combination of practical considerations and simple curiosity.

"You are strange, indeed," Jack repeated as he lit a cigarette and deeply inhaled its mentholated smoke.

"I may be strange, but I'm not suicidal," Frank replied in reference to his friend's addiction. Most of their friends smoked and Frank's abstinence was further evidence of his perverse detachment from the crowd, Jack thought but not in those exact words.

"I like living on the edge," was his response as he blew a puff of smoke at his friend, who barely noticed the toxic plume because the exhaust fan from the restaurant kitchen filled the alley around them with the heavy scent of Chinese cookery and who knew what else. There was also a bit of mist in the air, harbinger of a more substantial rain that had been predicted for later that evening. Frank was about to suggest they return to work when several sharp reports – muffled somewhat by the noisy exhaust fan – caught their attention.

"What was that?" Jack asked.

"Beats me, but it came from inside," Frank replied. They looked at each other for a moment and were about to dismiss the matter when the back door flew open and the entire kitchen staff – two Chinese men and a Mexican woman – fled the building and ran down the alley away from the restaurant. "Murder," one of the men yelled at the boys as he passed without further explanation.

Frank noticed that the door hung open, and there were no sounds he could detect from the kitchen. He went over to the doorway and cautiously peered into the room, which was predictably empty and devoid of the incessant chatter and clatter of pots and pans that usually filled the place.

"Let's get out of here," Jack insisted, taking a final drag on his cigarette and flipping the butt into the gathering darkness.

"I hear people in the dining room," Frank said, curious to know what was going on and wondering if anything had happened to those inside. He knew the people from the kitchen were safe, but Fletcher Woo as well as a bus boy, two waitresses and several dozen customers had been in the dining room when he and Jack took their breaks.

"Let's go," Jack urged, reluctant to follow his friend but somehow unable to desert him. Still reluctant, however, he followed Frank into the kitchen and a few minutes later through the swinging door into the dining room where clusters of people were milling about and others were visible on the sidewalk outside the main entrance to the restaurant. Frank's attention was immediately drawn to a man's body, sprawled on his back near the host's stand. He could not see the face, but knew instantly the victim was Fletcher Woo. He could tell by the gray suit and polished black shoes visible to him from across the room.

"Jesus," Jack said, arriving next to Frank a few moments later. He had never before been in the presence of death, not even a family funeral. They were to learn a little later that Woo was at his station near the front door, where he regularly greeted customers, when a man walked into the place and greeted him with several bullets to the chest. He fell dead to the floor as the killer left in the seconds before anyone realized what had happened.

Still later and after the crime had come under police investigation, Frank told Nick Satterfield what little he knew about the terrible event. "Fletcher's chickens came home to roost," was all Nick said in reply, aware there was not much chance the killer would be caught but completely unaware his remark would puzzle Frank for years to come.

*

Chapter Four

The smoke-like haze responsible for the name given the Great Smokey Mountains seemed more appropriate than usual as Frank Bonner piloted his yellow Stearman over the highest U.S. range east of the Mississippi River. Part of the Appalachian system, the heavily forested Smokies spread out under the Navy surplus flight trainer that Frank had purchased for $500 a month earlier. He was flying to his grandfather's funeral in Memphis from the small civilian airport near the large Marine Corps air base in North Carolina where he was stationed.

At 8,000 feet, the plane cruised somewhat below its normal 124 miles an hour speed as the result of a head wind, which at the time was the least of Corporal Bonner's problems. He knew he had crossed the Carolina line into Tennessee and was running low on fuel, but beyond that he had little notion of where he was in that vast wilderness. And the rugged terrain below him – unlike the flat landscape in Illinois where he had learned to fly – afforded no opportunity he could see for a comfortable emergency landing. "Crap," he thought to himself as he began to consider his limited options.

Built of wood, steel and fabric, the Boeing-Stearman was designed to train military pilots, and its rudimentary instrument panel served mainly to instruct those fliers on air speed, fuel consumption and other information that had little to do with the plane's geographic location. For navigation, Frank and many others in 1947 relied on something called Dead Reckoning, a form of guesswork that determined the position of an airplane from the record of its course, distance covered and the known or estimated drift. More confident than his experience justified, he had taken off with the notion a city as large as Memphis would surely not be all that difficult to find.

"I'm not going to jump out of this damn thing," he said aloud to himself, eliminating one of his main options, parachuting into what appeared to him an uninhabited and unending forest. He also realized his parachute was military surplus, which meant its age and condition were suspect. The chute had come with the plane and for all he knew it might be full of holes and tangled lines.

Frank began a gradual descent, maintaining a westerly heading and scanning the ground for the least suggestion of an open space that would accommodate his other principal option, an emergency landing. He didn't know or would have cared, given his predicament, that the Great Smokies were home to an incredible variety of trees and plants, not to mention black bears, other animals and birds. And while the regions coves and valleys had been sparsely settled since pioneer times, Frank could discern no signs of human life or an isolated meadow or field on which he might safely land his plane. He also noticed that the area's characteristic haze seemed to have intensified as he flew closer to the ground.

With no relatively safe options and his fuel indicator edging close to empty, Frank began to contemplate the prospect of settling the Stearman into the treetops when he spotted an intermittent blink of light, made visible during the day only by the gathered haze. He soon realized there was a rotating beacon of some sort that probably originated at an airport. "Why," he wondered, looking a gift horse directly in the mouth, "would anyone operate a beacon in broad daylight?" The answer to his question was more than apparent less than half an hour later when the light led him to an airport near Knoxville, where he landed the yellow biplane with barely enough fuel to taxi off the runway to a gas pump.

"No need to worry, Gram," he told his grandmother the next day when she learned he had flown his own plane to Memphis for the funeral. "The weather was good, and the airplane was great fun." He had not exactly lied, but assumed the full truth would have worried the woman, who had enough to deal with at the time. And while his flight from the coast to Knoxville had been a bit dicey, he had refueled there and made the rest of the trip without incident.

Frank's grandfather had been carried off by a sudden, massive coronary event in his early 60s. The whole family on Frank's paternal side – among them two aunts, their spouses and a variety of children, all younger than Frank – were surprised by the man's death, despite his long history of drinking and smoking.

Ed Bonner had been a physically imposing man, well over six feet tall at a time in human evolutionary history when most of his kind were considerably smaller. He had earned a living earlier as a horse trader and eventually owned a small trucking company, although he dabbled in a variety of enterprises that made him by his own account "comfortable." He drank a good deal of bourbon whisky on a regular basis, but never to the point where he was detectably drunk. And he smoked three packs of Twenty Grand cigarettes a day with no visible effect on his health, not, at least, until the day he dropped dead on a downtown street in his home town.

"He wasn't perfect but he was a good man," Frank's grandmother told him after the funeral and before she left for her home in the small Tennessee town where she lived and his dead father had grown up. He wasn't sure whether she meant his grandfather or his father, her long dead first born and favorite child.

"I won't, Gram," he promised, aware he wouldn't forget either of them, and suddenly recalling for no apparent reason he had never seen his grandfather in the winter. He recalled the man in neatly pressed short-sleeve shirts and seersucker pants because he had no recollection of him in cold weather. Frank's mother had dispatched him to visit his grandparents on summer vacations, never during the school year. He tried to imagine the old man in a fur-trimmed parka, but he couldn't evoke the image. He mainly remembered that his grandfather had promised him things over his childhood for later delivery. He had told him when he was about five he would buy him a shotgun when he was older, and had promised him at 10 that he'd get an old but operating Model A Ford when he reached legal driving age. Frank came to realize his grandfather had made these promises simply to shut him up, and had given these matters no further thought. He didn't understand, Frank realized, that children often have long term memories which are quite at odds with the short attention spans for which they are often noted. "Don't lie to a kid," was the lesson Frank took from this realization.

"We don't see you often enough, Frankie," were the last words his grandmother said to him after the funeral and before one of his uncles drove him to the airport where he had parked the Stearman the previous day. She had asked him to spend time with her and the family in the small Tennessee town where Bonners had lived for a number of generations, but he begged off on the pretext his military leave time was limited. That was true to some extent, but he didn't tell her he planned to fly on to St. Louis to see his girlfriend. He also didn't tell her he had flown to the funeral mainly as an excuse to eventually spend time with Molly.

"I hate weddings and funerals," Frank had confessed to Private First Class Jack Smiley at the Marine Corps air base before he began the trip. The two friends had been together since their enlistments, recruit training and assignments to a Marine air wing.

"Then why go?" Jack inquired, fully aware Frank's motivation was to some minor extent family obligation supplemented by the more important opportunities to fly the Stearman cross country and to visit Molly.

"There's a spare seat in the airplane," Frank had offered, equally aware Jack knew the answer to his own question. He also knew his friend would not likely accept the offer of a free ride to St. Louis or anywhere else in an airplane.

"You couldn't get me in that rickety old pile of flying junk if you got me laid on a daily basis by the babe of my choice," Jack said. He recalled the short plane ride at the small Illinois airport and the lunch he had pitched just off the runway. The prospect of bouncing around in an open cockpit for several hours had little appeal for him even though he now worked in a maintenance capacity for a military aircraft squadron. "I don't mind fixing the damned things, but I don't intend to fly around in some freakin' mechanical contraption," he added. "Too many moving parts too far off the ground."

As Frank flew north from Memphis – mainly tracking the Mississippi River, which was going the other way – he thought about his father's family, and realized he was mainly indifferent to them with the single exception of his grandmother. He wondered for a few moments why he felt no familial attachment to that particular assembly of relatives and finally chalked his feelings up to their general lack of contact over the years. He liked the various aunts, uncles and cousins well enough, but they simply weren't important to him. He also suspected he wasn't important to them, which probably had some considerable influence on his attitude. "Screw 'em," he thought and turned his attention to his immediate destination.

The sky was unusually clear – even over the drab industrial areas that lined the river on the Illinois side across from St. Louis – when Frank banked the Stearman a bit east toward the familiar airport now called Hager Field. Before long, he could see the arc of the familiar lake, although it was seasonally devoid of the waterfowl that used it as a stop-over on annual migrations along the ancient Mississippi flyway. Otherwise, the airport had not changed in the past few years and neither had Bill Hager, who had watched the yellow Stearman land and was curious to see who was in it. By the time Frank had taxied up to the low fence that served as a make-shift flight line, the older man was there to inspect the plane. He was in the market for a Stearman and had no idea this one was piloted by one of his former students.

“Hi, Bill,” Frank said as he hauled himself out of the cockpit and gingerly used a lower wing to reach the ground next to a puzzled Bill Hager, who knew he was confronted by a familiar face but couldn’t quite complete the identification. “I’m Frank Bonner,” he added to clear up the obvious mystery.

“I never thought otherwise,” Hager lied, shaking the younger man’s hand. “I thought you were in the Army.”

“The Marine Corps,” Frank corrected. He wore an old pair of khaki pants and a worn leather flight jacket, which was almost a uniform at many small airports where the occasional former military pilot either worked or hung out in the years immediately following the war. His own forest green uniform, which would have identified his branch of service, was neatly folded and packed in a blue canvas bag with his toilet articles and a change of socks and underwear.

Hager’s memory of Frank was soon restored and the two men got into a discussion about the Stearman, which the airport proprietor inspected like some old rancher who was checking out a prize bull he intended to buy. Telling Frank about everything from his recent purchase of a partner’s half interest in the airport to the poor state of his health, he scrutinized the plane from nose to tail and from its wings to its big fixed wheels. “You want to sell this thing?” he said at last to Frank, who had thought the man’s interest in his aircraft was only a matter of simple curiosity. “I hadn’t given it any thought,” Frank replied.

“I’ll give you eight hundred dollars for it,” Hager offered, guessing correctly the amount exceeded the price Frank had paid for the plane.

“I flew in from the Carolinas and I don’t want to take the bus back, Frank said with some truthfulness, but without admitting he'd gotten lost over the eastern mountains.

"How about six hundred dollars and my 1936 Plymouth," Hager suggested. "The car is in mint condition and you can drive back to the Carolinas." The car, he knew, wasn't in mint condition, but it ran well enough and would probably make it to the coast.

Frank was about to decline the offer when the prospect of a profit and a car made him seriously consider the offer. The car, too, would relieve him of the need to cross those mountains again, at least until he had more navigation experience. The fresh recollection of all those trees taught him a valuable lesson, and Hager's offer provided, he now realized, an opportunity not to repeat his earlier mistake. "I'd like to see the car," he said.

The old automobile - which Hager had intended to sell in any event – looked pretty good to Frank, who noticed it had recently been cleaned and polished. He also noticed the worn upholstery, but figured new seat covers would remedy that defect so long as the machine ran well, which it did. He drove it up and down the adjacent state road with Hager in the passenger seat to make that discovery for himself and then, when they returned to the airport, agreed to sell his plane. "It's a deal and I'll throw in the chute," Frank told Hager, who got the joke because he knew the worth of surplus parachutes.

Frank loved the Stearman, but he was a pragmatic young man who realized he could use the car to take his girlfriend, Molly, out in something other than a bus or streetcar while he was in St. Louis, and later drive the machine east where he could sell it to someone on the military base. With luck, he could eventually net several hundred dollars on the sale of his plane. "Not too bad," he thought as he drove away from the airport, his canvas traveling bag on the seat next to him and thoughts of his girlfriend, who he had not seen in six months, on his mind.

"I've met someone else," Molly told Frank, her voice soft and confidential. They were sitting in his car outside her apartment building after an evening out in which she had been unusually restrained.

"So have I," he replied, aware of what she meant but deferring the inevitable with an attempt at levity. "I've met a bunch of someone elses."

"You know what I mean," she said quietly.

"You mean you're dumping me for someone you like better."

"No, I'm exchanging you for someone who wants to get married," Molly explained.

"I can't afford to get married, not now," Frank pointed out. "I've still got another year on my Marine Corps hitch and three or four years of college before that's anywhere near possible."

"That's the point," she said, grasping his sleeve and gently pulling him toward her for what she intended as a parting kiss. That intention, however, hadn't taken into account the attraction that had brought them together in the first place, and they were soon engaged in the series of intimacies that had once been confined to the apartment building stairway. Puzzled by the contradiction, Frank was even more mystified by the first words she spoke when their lips separated after a particularly intense kiss. "Do you want me?" she inquired.

"Pardon me?" was all he could think to say.

"Would you like to do it with me?" Molly essentially repeated, this time in words he immediately understood.

She had realized his car made possible something that was not impossible but entirely too risky in their old hallway setting.

"Damn right," he said and kissed her again, drawing her as close as the automobile's long floor shift would allow and wondering if his response had been a little too blatant for the occasion. Apparently not, he decided a moment later when she withdrew from the kiss to suggest they go somewhere that afforded more privacy.

Somewhat later, Frank and Molly lay awkwardly naked in the back seat of the old Plymouth, their bodies partially illuminated by pale moonlight and their clothes hung over the back of the front seats. The act had been consummated to their mutual satisfaction, even though it was the first time for both of them. He had found a secluded place in the vast city park he had wandered as a boy, a park whose geography was as familiar to him as the neighborhood in which he had lived through most of his childhood.

"Does this mean we're okay?" Frank asked after a long period in which neither of them said a word.

"We're just fine, but I'm still getting married," Molly replied, and went on to explain she wanted a family and didn't want to wait until she was an old woman to have one. The back of her head was nestled on his chest and his arms were folded about her with his hands gently covering her breasts against the cool night air.

"You're 19 years old, for Christ's sake," he pointed out despite his confidence she was aware of the fact. "You've probably got another three or four years before you die of old age."

"And you've got another three or four years before you even think about marriage, and there's no telling what you'll be thinking about then," she said. She almost told him not to use The Lord's name in vain, but decided a small moral lecture was inappropriate, given the general situation.

"Who's the lucky guy?" he asked after another prolonged silence. Eventually, however, she divulged the name of someone he didn't know, someone he didn't like even though he didn't know him. Soon afterward, they dressed and he took her home, said goodbye and drove out of her life with the conviction he would never see her again. He was sadder than he had been since his father's death, but eventually learned that time – in this case a couple of months – would dissipate his sense of loss. But he would neither forget Molly and their final evening together nor understand why she gave him at the end of their relationship what she had previously withheld. He didn't know that Molly was left with the same kind of recollection and the same question.

"I want you to have this," Nick Satterfield said to Frank and carefully handed him an old but meticulously maintained .45 caliber automatic pistol. "I've had this since the First War and it's saved my bacon a couple of times." Frank – who had been dumped the night before by Molly and would leave the following day for North Carolina – had just had dinner with his mother, who was washing dishes, and Nick. The two men were in another room, out of earshot of Sally Satterfield, who, Nick knew, would not have approved the gift.

"Thank you," Frank said for lack of a more adequate way of expressing appreciation for something he knew Nick had kept and prized for a long time. He took the gun and measured its heft while admiring a weapon that had been adopted by the Marine Corps in 1913.

"You'd better put that away before your mother sees it," Nick advised, aware by the way Frank handled the gun that he knew what he was doing. Frank, he also knew, had qualified as a sharpshooter during his basic Marine training, which was the highest rating he could have achieved and was the result of his single-minded application to that particular task and his extraordinary eyesight. Nick would not have given him the pistol without the reassurance of that knowledge.

"I think you know I don't believe in killing, people or anything else," Nick explained, "but there are times when you need to protect yourself."

"I understand," Frank replied, and he did. Nick had expressed his opinion many times about the futility of violence, although he had never said a word to Frank about his long and bitter experiences in the First World War. Frank, however, had put two and two together and gotten four. He didn't know the precise nature of those experiences but he knew there was a connection between the war and Nick's strongly held views about the random use of force. "I promise not to shoot anyone who doesn't deserve it," he said and went off to stow the .45 in his canvas traveling bag.

Frank thought about his mother and Nick the next day as he drove the old Plymouth across one of the Mississippi River bridges into Illinois and headed southeast toward North Carolina. "Not tonight, Nick, not with Frank in the apartment," he had overheard his mother tell her husband after they had gone to bed. Not yet tired enough to sleep, Frank was in the nearby living room reading an article in a news magazine about the first pilot to break the sound barrier. Momentarily distracted by his mother's voice, he realized that his presence had kept Nick from getting laid that evening. "That's a lousy way to show my appreciation for the gun," he thought, amused for a moment before he returned his attention to the article.

Air Force Captain Charles Yeager had flown the experimental Bell X-1 at supersonic speed on October 14 as part of a research program at the Muroc Army Air Field where he was a test pilot, Frank learned. He also read that Yeager was a World War Two ace credited with 11.5 kills, including one of the first air-to-air victories over a German jet fighter.

The article told Frank the historic test flight was made at 45,000 feet, but it didn't tell him that Yeager had broken two ribs a couple of days earlier and was in such pain before take-off that he couldn't seal the plane's hatch by himself. He managed that rudimentary task with a broom handle rigged for him by a friend.

Yeager – who flew P-51 Mustangs during the war – was shot down over France on his eighth mission in 1944, but escaped to Spain with the help of the French Resistance and eventually made his way back to England where he was reinstated for further combat service. He subsequently distinguished himself by becoming what they called an "ace in a day," which meant he shot down five enemy aircraft on a single mission. He achieved two of those kills without firing a shot when he flew into firing position against a German pilot who apparently panicked and veered his Messerschmitt into a wingman.

Frank's modest military career and limited flight experience were in no way comparable to the intrepid fighter and test pilot, but he and Yeager had at least one thing in common. They both had extraordinary vision, and Yeager's keen eyesight, according to the article, had been an important factor in his success as a fighter pilot. The piece also alleged Yeager had once shot a deer at 600 yards, which was only a little further than the 500 yard targets Frank had consistently bulls-eyed on the rifle range at Marine boot camp. Frank knew he was no Chuck Yeager – who he thought about from time to time as he drove through Illinois and Kentucky into Tennessee – but he took some pride in their one similarity. With little else to occupy his time, he occasionally put his vision to the test. He peered into the distance to see what he could see.

The device – along with his thoughts about Chuck Yeager and other random things – was a way to avoid thinking about Molly, who he missed more and more as the distance between them increased with the mileage on his car. He wondered if he had made a mistake by not asking her to marry him, either earlier or when he discovered she had met someone else. "I can't get married now," he told himself time and again to dispel the recollection of his loss.

Somewhere east of Knoxville, Frank discerned a hitchhiker in the distance and decided to give him a ride as payback to the drivers who had picked him up when he had thumbed rides from the base to nearby towns. "It's the least I can do," he thought and pulled off the road ahead of a tall, thin man who soon caught up to him as the car braked to a stop. "Where are you going?" he asked the stranger once he had occupied the front passenger seat.

"Asheville," the man replied and then lapsed into silence. Frank noticed that his new companion was extraordinarily pale and without baggage of any kind. Strange, he thought, for someone alone in the mountains. These were roughly the same mountains – part of the great Appalachian chain that extended from Canada into the southern United States – he had crossed flying west some days earlier in the Stearman.

This time, however, he had a fair notion of where he was and where he was going, a thought he found amusing until the hitchhiker broke his chain of thought. "I want your money and your car," he said in a voice that was barely discernable. Frank looked at him and discovered the man held a long, switchblade knife, which he used to indicate he wanted the car pulled onto the road shoulder.

"Are you sure?" Frank inquired in a level voice that surprised the knife wielder, who had expected a reaction somewhere between nervousness and panic.

"Pull the fucking car over or I'll carve you like a Christmas goose," the man ordered as Frank slowed the Plymouth down and gradually eased off the highway onto a gravel bed that crunched under its weight. "Get out," he added when they had come to a complete stop.

"I don't think so," Frank said. "Open the door and ditch the knife." The would-be robber was astounded to discover a large pistol pointed directly at his head from a scant two feet away. Frank had stashed the .45 in the small crevice between the door and the driver's seat, where he had instant access to it once the need became apparent.

"Easy, man," the hitchhiker urged, and did what he was told. His pallid face had turned a bit paler.

"Get out, leave the door open and keep your hands where I can see 'em," Frank further instructed the hitchhiker, who followed his orders but whose worried expression showed he had no idea of what to expect. Frank followed him across the bench-type seat and out of the car where the two men stood face-to-face. "What's your name?" he asked.

"Glen," the hitchhiker replied.

" Glen what?"

"Glen Higgins," he instinctively lied.

"Well, Glen Higgins," Frank said, extending the gun at arm's length in the direction of the hitchhiker's head, "I've got some good news and some bad news for you." The man stared at him blankly, unsure of what he meant until Frank clarified his intentions. "I'm not going to shoot your sorry head off," he added. "That's the good news." About to plead his case, the hitchhiker got the bad news before he could utter a word. Frank struck him hard in the face with the barrel of his gun, landing a solid blow that broke his jaw and sent him reeling down an embankment away from the road. He lay there, either unconscious or feigning it, in a crumpled heap, where Frank left him and drove away.

At the time, Frank didn't realize the experience had released a long submerged hatred – traceable to the death of his father at the hands of murderous felons – that suddenly surfaced at the expense of the hitchhiker. As he steered east toward North Carolina, the full reality of what he had done slowly crept into his thoughts. He had left a man, probably unconscious, in a mountainside ditch late in October with little to shield him from the weather. And he had done it without the slightest hesitation and no lingering remorse.

"The bastard deserved what he got," Frank concluded, and switched his headlights on as darkness gathered about the old Plymouth.

*

Chapter Five

"I bloody well told you to stay out of the reserves when we were discharged," Frank told Jack Smiley as they had morning coffee in the small backroom of The Outpost and counted receipts from the night before. "The pittance they pay you isn't worth the hassle."

"I needed the money," Jack replied. "Who'd have guessed we'd be in another war so soon." His reference was to the North Korean invasion of South Korea earlier that summer and to the subsequent dispatch of U.S. ground forces to the area. The two young men had been mustered out of the regular Marine Corps in 1948, two years earlier, but Jack had joined the reserves and was now facing a call-up to active duty. "I don't care if those communist bastards invade Minnesota, I'm not going back in service," he said, aware his threat was as hollow as a long dead tree trunk and that there was little he could do about the gathering of world events.

"If it's any comfort, you don't need the money now," Frank observed, pointing to the stacks of bills, mostly ones, fives, 10s and 20s on the desk between them. They had opened the beer hall several months after their enrollments at the state university with several thousand dollars Frank had saved during his tour of duty in the Corps. They had purchased a small land parcel just outside the university town, and erected a surplus Army barracks now furnished with an odd assortment of heavily used tables and chairs that seemed to match the rough wooden booths and small bar the two men had built with the help of cheap student labor.

"It's not much comfort, but what the hell," Jack said as they banded the stacks of money that would be deposited later that morning in a local bank. The Outpost – where they sold several brands of domestic beer, one on tap and the others in long neck bottles – had developed an immediate student following and had enabled the two entrepreneurs to retire the small debt they had assumed to open the place. They subsequently installed a grill where they cooked two kinds of hamburgers – one with cheese and the other without – and dispensed a large selection of chips and other packaged foods that were mainly devoid of nutrition.

"It's almost like stealing," Jack thought and put the banded bills into a canvas bag he would soon take to the bank, but not before he opened the front and only door for business. It was mid-morning and a few of their customers – mostly student veterans of the recent World War – would arrive before long for hamburgers and beer, their concept of a hardy breakfast. Financed by a government program popularly called the G.I. Bill of Rights, these former soldiers, sailors and marines gave the university environment a somewhat more mature aspect than was apparent before the end of hostilities. They were older than the students who had not seen military service and many of them were easily identified by the government-issued khaki pants they wore year-round.

Frank had recruited his trusted friend, Jack, as a partner in the business because common sense told him some employees would steal from him if left to their own devices. He knew two pairs of eyes were preferable to one in a beer hall as surely as they were in the cockpits of combat aircraft. As it turned out, Jack not only liked the enterprise but had a genuine gift for its management and the resourcefulness to handle daily problems that would otherwise have plagued Frank. "You're not entirely useless," Frank once advised Jack, who took it as the compliment his partner had intended.

The summer semesters at the University – usually tranquil compared with the rest of the bustling year – had been transformed with the influx of military veterans seeking higher education and lives beyond the battlefields. The student population had soared following the war and residents of the town could no longer expect the relative serenity that previous summers had brought them. With the exception of a few weeks in August when summer school had ended and the new term had not yet begun, the community had all the aspects of a boom town. The natives were generally put off by this turbulence, but the two beer hall proprietors had stumbled into a business environment that soon gave them respectable bank accounts and a sense of independence that was abruptly diminished in early July when Jack was ordered to report for active duty with the Marine Corps. The Korean War had caught up with him.

"Son of a bitch," was Jack's initial reaction to his call up, even though it had not been unexpected. He knew the nation had demobilized its military forces after the Second World War and that reservists would surely be employed to fill the gap until new troops could be gathered and trained. He had brought the bad news back to The Outpost that evening, and the partners sat in the small office discussing the situation.

"I'll look after the business until you get back, which I expect will be soon," Frank said. He meant the part about the business but had serious reservations as far as the time frame for hostilities was concerned. He knew enough not to predict the duration of wars.

"I don't see why they didn't call you," Jack said in a feeble effort to amuse himself and ignoring the reality that Frank wasn't a reservist. "You're in better shape for all that military crap." The real joke lay in his knowledge that Frank was in better shape for almost anything. He had since his mid-teens combined weight and martial arts training to the point where his strength was apparent to anyone who bothered to notice. He made no effort to display his accumulated muscles – preferring, instead, loose fitting clothes – but his flat facial planes, devoid of fat, and wide shoulders provided a hint, at least, of his substantial strength. There was no indication, however, of the martial arts skills he had acquired under the assumption that effort would one day serve some real purpose. He had studied several disciplines, including karate and judo, and had mingled those skills into the ability to physically defeat much larger opponents, including competent boxers, wrestlers and plain street fighters. And while he tried as a matter of personal policy to avoid conflict, his ownership of a business that transformed some young men into surly drunks ensured that commendable intention was all but impossible.

"I'll beat you to a bloody pulp," one bleary-eyed but rather large lineman on the school's football team had boasted some months earlier when Frank had cut off his beer supply on grounds he'd had enough. The situation wasn't all that uncommon and rarely led to anything other than temporary disgruntlement on the part of the expelled customers, who usually forgot the episodes and were back at The Outpost a few nights later. But this particular drunk persisted and attempted an assault on Frank, who put him down in an instant before a large customer audience whose subsequent recitations of the event contributed to the proprietor's reputation for toughness and reduced the number of future confrontations.

The unmistakable rumble of multiple motorcycles was a momentary distraction for Frank and Jack as they continued a discussion of the changes the new war would impose on their lives and on the business. They were barely aware the bikers – five in all – had pulled onto their gravel parking lot and entered the building through the only door, which one of the two student employees, who had run the bar that evening, was about to shut. "Sorry," he said to the lead biker, "we're closing for the night."

"Not yet," the man, who wore a red bandana tied about his head and a worn leather vest, said and rudely pushed him aside. The others swaggered behind him into the room and soon crowded the small bar. "Beer," one of them yelled and pounded on the counter top to make his point.

"I'll check with the owner," the second student, who had witnessed everything from his perch on a stool near the grill, replied, and retreated to the nearby office door, which he opened a bit. "We've got a bunch of goons out here, and they won't let us close the place," he whispered into the office to Frank and Jack, who got the message. They soon emerged into the main room to confront the visitors, whose raucous chatter had an aura of unruliness about it. “Is there a problem?” Frank inquired in a voice loud enough to get their attention.

“We want something to drink,” the leader responded in a raspy voice that suggested there was little room for negotiation.

“We’re closed,” Frank said.

“Then there’s a problem,” the biker explained.

“Maybe, but it’s your problem,” Frank advised and produced the old .45 caliber pistol he had retrieved from his desk drawer and concealed until that moment behind his back. He made certain the gun was plainly visible but didn’t point it at anyone. “Now get your scraggily asses out of here and don’t come back.”

“You’re a big man with that gun, aren’t you?” the lead biker inquired. His friends had gone quiet once the weapon had been produced.

“Big enough, with or without the gun,” Frank said and surprised him with an offer he hadn’t expected. “Would you like to go a few rounds with me one on one?’

“Any day,” the biker replied, forgetting that night had long since fallen. He was taller and heavier than Frank, but hadn’t bothered to measure the man he was about to fight. He seemed a rough sort who had probably battled his way through much of life and would have accepted the challenge from anyone.

“Outside, then,” Frank instructed everyone, mindful of the furniture he needed to run the business, and then followed the gang to the parking lot with Jack and the two students behind him. “Watch my back,” he said to Jack and handed him the .45.

“If anyone gives me a problem, where should I shoot them?” Jack asked Frank.

“Aim for the dick,” Frank advised. He almost said “groin,” but figured the other word would make the point more plainly.

The biker’s gang backed him, as if on cue, and Jack and the student employees assembled on the other side, leaving the two combatants to face one another in the pale moonlight. A soft breeze rustled through the mature trees along one of the property lines and an owl could be heard in the distance.

“You’re gonna regret this,” the lead biker said to Frank with undisguised contempt for what he thought was a really stupid gesture. He still wore his rough leather gloves, which he assumed would inflict considerable damage on the man who now took his measure.

“I doubt it, but let’s find out,” Frank replied as the biker suddenly lunged in his direction, only to sweep past a target that eluded him with barely perceptible motion. He then repeated the charge several times with the same effect, his anger and frustration apparently rising all the time. “Stand still, you freakin’ sissy,” he yelled at last and advanced slowly with his large fists tightly clenched. This time, Frank stood his ground, ducked under the inevitable punch, and delivered a kick to the man’s groin that doubled him over into a hand chop that broke his nose. The blows put the biker flat on his back, where he lay with blood flowing from his nostrils.

He remained on the gravel for a moment, gathering muddled thoughts, and then got up, mopping his bloody nose with a shirtsleeve. It was obvious to everyone there he intended to continue the fight, but his apparent anger was no longer visible and he now seemed to anticipate a contest he had previously considered no contest at all.

Frank, meanwhile, watched him carefully and decided to end the match in a way that would avoid the inconvenience of ambulances and police cars. Oddly, too, he felt no real anger toward the biker who he considered no more than a minor nuisance and who now faced him again.

"Try this on for size," the biker said with the intention of breaking something on Frank's face. Instead, he missed again and took two rapid strokes to the head that sent him reeling to the ground, where he lay, this time on his side, unconscious. His gang and the two students looked on in something that approached amazement, but Jack had anticipated the outcome. "Don't screw with my partner," he announced, scratching the side of his head with the barrel of the .45 as the biker slowly regained consciousness. "You win," he said to Frank after a while and got up. "Where did you learn that stuff?"

Frank ignored the question, but made an offer in a spontaneous gesture that surprised everyone there. "I'll buy a round of beers if you put them down in a hurry and get the hell out of here." It was an offer they couldn't refuse.

Before the five men finished their drinks and rode off into the summer night, however, Frank and Jack were surprised to learn they were not the gang of renegade bikers they had sought to portray. They were rowdy enough – mainly the result of too many earlier beers – but all were faculty members in the University history department and the lead biker was a full professor, PHD and all. His given name was Reginald Finney III and he taught a course for graduate students called "The Italian Renaissance, Prelude to Pizza." Finney had introduced himself to Frank as he drank the one beer allotment and carefully dabbed at his nose with the headband he formerly wore. "You really beat the crap out of me, although I don't remember most of it," he admitted with what struck Frank as a good natured attitude. Frank subsequently began to suspect the man's apparent anger during their one-sided tussle had been an act, something he did for amusement or diversion that had nothing to do with his true feelings. "If that's the case, he's probably tough enough to get away with it most of the time," Frank thought as he and Jack dismissed the two students for the night and locked the only door behind them.

Two weeks later, Jack was on his way to the west coast to join the 1st Marine Division and Frank had purchased a two-place airplane for a flight to Mexico. They had sold The Outpost to Dr. Finney, who not only turned out to be a somewhat eccentric academic but a wealthy one as well. Something about the beer hall had caught his fancy, and he called Frank a few days after their meeting with an offer to buy the place. In less than two years, the partners had worked their way into respectable money, which they split down the middle. "Stay alive," Frank instructed Jack when he drove him to the depot where he boarded a westward bound train for the long haul to California.

Frank's interest in Mexico had developed some months earlier when he read two books, William Prescott's "The Conquest of Mexico" and "The Conquest of New Spain." written by Bernal Diaz. Prescott, who died in 1859 at 63, was a blind historian who told the story of a small band of ruthless Spanish adventurers under command of Hernan Cortez who destroyed the powerful Aztec empire. The Spaniards embarked for Mexico in 1519 and assumed control of the country two years later. Prescott drew a good deal of his material from the book by Diaz, who served under Cortez and wrote his account 50 years after the event, which may have been one of the most daring military feats in history. The Spaniards, like the Aztecs they defeated, had their cruel aspect, but Frank knew enough not to let his modern notions pass judgment on those who lived in an entirely different time and in other circumstances. He simply found the whole story incredibly interesting and wanted to see the places where it happened.

As fall approached, Frank prepared for the trip south with flights around the state in his newly acquired Cessna 120 to familiarize himself with the aircraft. Although the plane had room for a single passenger, he would make the long passage alone at cruising speeds just above 100 miles an hour and altitudes well below the craft's 15,000 foot service ceiling. And since the 120's range was about 400 miles and it wasn't equipped with a radio, let alone the avionics or lights for nighttime flights – just as Frank had not yet qualified to pilot anything after dark – the trip was destined to take some time, which was actually part of the plan. There were places along the way where Frank intended to stop, both for fuel, food and to relieve his bladder as well as to hang out for a couple of days if he found anything of interest. Anything at all.

"What to do?" Frank thought, as he saw the incredibly dark clouds with occasional strokes of lightning off to the west between him and his home airport. He had flown to St. Louis to visit his mother and Nick Satterfield a month before his departure for Mexico and had expected an uneventful return flight. The bad weather had been unpredicted – at least to his knowledge - and he soon realized that stormy conditions had also broken out around him. Although still in clear air, he was almost encircled by some of the nastiest stuff he had ever seen and soon decided to seek safety on the ground.

Frank's concept of an emergency landing had always centered on a large meadow free of plowed furrows or tall crops, but nothing of that kind was available as large wet drops began to splatter against his windscreen, precursors of the storm. At that moment, he spotted a long, straight dirt road, empty of traffic, off to his left and stretching into the distance. Only a few hundred feet above the ground by that time, he slipped the plane into alignment with the improvised runway and set it down on a surface that proved to be surprisingly smooth for something that had mainly accommodated trucks and various kinds of farm equipment. "Neat job, Bonner," Frank said to himself, as he taxied onto a narrow strip of adjacent grass and switched off the engine as a hard rain descended on the stationary Cessna and its relieved pilot.

"Buenos Dias, senor," the shepherd greeted Frank, who had fitfully slept the night away in the cockpit of his plane when the storm raged on well past sundown. The man, wearing a serape and surrounded by a flock of sheep on the nearby road, seemed unsurprised that an airplane was parked where it was. But Frank was unaccustomed to Spanish-speaking sheep herders in the nation's heartland. Migrant workers of various sorts, perhaps, but not sheep herders. "Buenos Dias," he never-the-less replied, exhausting most of the Spanish at his disposal.

Stiffened by what amounted to a long nap in the cramped cockpit, Frank got out of the 120 and made his way through milling sheep to the shepherd. He wondered if the man could provide some clue to his precise location – even though he was not lost - and he also wanted to test the roadway to make certain the heavy rain had not rendered it too soft for a take-off. As he soon learned, the shepherd spoke not a word of English, but the hard-packed road had shed water like the proverbial duck's back and was suitable, barring unexpected traffic, for an early escape from what turned out to be no predicament at all.

The two men spoke to each other – one in English and the other in Spanish – for several minutes and to little avail, although they both seemed to agree it was a splendid fall morning with clear skies and no sign of the storm that had recently drenched the landscape. "Adios, mi amigo," the shepherd said at last when Frank returned to the plane, which he carefully inspected from the outside before he strapped himself into the cockpit seat, started the engine and let it warm up as he checked the instrument panel. The man and his sheep, meanwhile, stayed where they were until Frank had taxied onto the road ahead of them, revved his engine in a final test, and then roared down this rural runway for a mere 500 feet before he was airborne. As he gained altitude in a shallow bank toward home, Frank looked back at the diminishing shepherd, who stood among his sheep and waved at him. "Adios," Frank said aloud.

A month later, Frank was stuck at a small airport in northeast Texas, where he had sought refuge from still another rainstorm on the second day of his flight to Mexico. He had left his home base in clear, late fall weather and flown southwest out of Missouri, clipping a small section of northwest Arkansas and into eastern Oklahoma, where he spent the first night in a cheap motel near an airport with paved runways. He took off early the next morning with the intention of reaching the Dallas area later that day, but was forced down before noon by a weather front that arrived somewhat earlier than the forecasts had suggested.

The airport was little more than a cow pasture with a single hangar and a surplus military building that served as an office for the field's owner-operator, a raw-boned, middle aged Texan who helped Frank tie the Cessna down against the rising wind and heavy raindrops that preceded the main storm. They had barely secured the plane and reached shelter when the full force of Mother Nature arrived with sufficient wind and water to obscure the half dozen aircraft, including Frank's plane, that bobbed up and down against the lines that kept them from blowing away. "I'm James," the Texan remarked as they entered the office, "not Jim, Jimmy, Jamie or Jimbo."

"I'm Bob," Frank replied, thinking there was no particular reason James needed to know his real name.

"This should blow out of here pretty soon," James observed in reference to the weather as he motioned Frank to seat himself on a worn-out couch next to a table that supported an ancient two-way radio and an ashtray full of cigarette butts. He took the only other seat in the room, an armless wooden chair that served his desk.

"How soon?" Frank inquired.

"I'd guess an hour or so, judging by the weather report," James said. Frank wondered where he got the weather report, given the sparseness of equipment in the building, but put the thought aside to inquire about nearby restaurants. He was hungry and wasn't particularly interested in hanging around the airport until the weather improved.

"There's only one," James informed him, "and that's

Big Joe's Bar-B-Q just down the road. The food ain't anything special, but it won't kill you right off."

"Swell," Frank thought, but asked if there was any kind of transportation, given the pouring rain, that could take him to the place.

"Only me," James said, "but you're in luck. I can work you into my busy schedule, which is to say I'll drive you to Big Joe's in my truck. Call me when you're ready to come back and I'll pick you up." Frank accepted the offer, and soon discovered that "just down the road" was, indeed, just down the road. Big Joe's was no more than a couple of hundred yards from the airport office, an easy stroll had the weather not been so stormy. As it turned out, the short ride in James' vintage Chevy pick-up – probably something from the mid-30s, Frank judged – was only a little drier than a walk would have been. The window on the passenger side was jammed two-thirds of the way up, and Frank got a short shower during the ride from the airport to a concrete block building with a large window full of neon beer signs. But he was grateful for the lift and thanked James, who gave him a worn match cover with his phone number scrawled on the blank interior.

Inside, Frank discovered a rough but surprisingly large room with booths down one wall and more tables and chairs than the population of the area was likely to need. The bar, too, seemed longer than necessary and appeared somewhat barren, given the absence of liquor bottles on an empty shelf behind it. Had he been interested enough to ask, Frank would have learned the sale of anything other than beer was prohibited by law in that jurisdiction.

"Some weather, huh?" the bartender greeted him as he deposited his wet jacket on the back of a barstool and sat down. Frank guessed the man was none other than Big Joe, judging by his enormous size and proprietary manner. The guess was rendered moot when the man introduced himself. "I'm Big Joe," he said. "What's your name?"

"Bob," Frank replied.

"Welcome to the boondocks, Bob." Joe's remark implied he knew a stranger when he met one, particularly one from a more populated part of the country. "What's your poison?"

"Make it a burger and a cup of black coffee," Frank said, skipping his preference for a beer because he intended to fly out of the place as soon as the weather cleared. Joe took the order but lingered a while for conversation with the stranger. He was both curious and friendly by nature, and those character traits usually won out over business considerations. "Where are you headed?" he asked.

"Dallas," Frank told him with some reluctance and without divulging his ultimate destination, Mexico. He didn't tell him his intention was to bi-pass Dallas and other large metropolitan areas and to fly south on a track that would skirt Austin, San Antonio and Laredo in Texas. Once over the border, he planned to continue south past Monterrey, San Luis Potosi and Mexico City to a small mountain airport somewhat beyond the old mining town turned tourist trap, Taxco. He had researched the entire route and located the small, out of the way air fields that seemed more compatible with his lack of electronic equipment.

"Business or pleasure?" Joe persisted.

"Both," Frank lied, wondering what it would take to get the curious bartender to order his food. He was pondering that matter when a woman's voice broke his train of thought. “You want company?” he heard her ask before he turned to discover a small, almost girlish person in blue jeans and a tight red sweater standing behind him.

“Get your trouble-making ass out of here,” Joe told her before Frank could answer the question.

“That’s no way to talk to a lady,” she responded with a mock smile.

“I ain’t talkin’ to a lady,” Joe said. It was apparent to Frank and to any one of the several other men seated down the bar that these two were not at odds with one another for the first time. Frank figured the others – probably regular customers – were familiar with the problem, which he soon understood when an angry young man strode up to the bar and launched an abusive tirade at him. “Who in hell gave you the right to hit on my woman?” he screamed at Frank, who thought at first he was yelling at Joe. “I’ll bust your face if you don’t get lost,” he continued. He was stocky enough to make the threat plausible and the rage written on his face was a clear indication of his intention to do what he had threatened.

“Take it easy, Freddie,” Joe advised the young man as his girl friend sidled closer to Frank in an obvious effort to further annoy her boyfriend. The two had argued and the woman sought to make him jealous, a device that had caused trouble in Big Joe’s bar on several other occasions.

“You take it easy,” Freddie said and pushed the woman away from Frank, who had swiveled on his barstool to confront the young man. They were almost nose to nose when Frank planted the sole of his shoe on the man’s stomach and gently but firmly pushed him away. “You don’t want to do this,” he warned, aware nothing he said would make any difference.

"Screw you," Freddie shouted, his fist cocked to strike Frank as he stepped squarely into a solid punch that had nothing to do with the martial arts. Frank had simply delivered a hard blow to the mouth that sent his assailant to the floor where he lay stretched out in a position reminiscent of crucifixion. The punch had loosened a few teeth, but Freddie had been rendered unconscious when his head hit the floor with a thud heard down the bar.

"Jesus," Big Joe said, "I hope you didn't kill the fool." He then advised Frank to leave the place and explained that the young man he had just put down was the local sheriff's son. "He knows the boy isn't worth much, but he's still his father," Joe added. And as Frank, still hungry, took his advice, the big man came around the bar, hoisted the trouble-making girl friend over his shoulder and took her, screaming and futilely beating at his back, to a rear door where he tossed her out of the building. "Good riddance," were the last words Frank heard him say as he collected his jacket, left by the front door and jogged off to the airport under a clearing sky.

James was surprised to see Frank so soon, but he was the kind of man who tended his own business and didn't inquire into the affairs of others, particularly those he barely knew. Instead, he helped Frank release the tie-down lines that had secured the plane during the storm and to refuel the aircraft before his customer paid the bill in cash and taxied out onto the field. The Cessna remained for some time, engine idling, while Frank carefully consulted charts before he finally took off, climbed to sufficient altitude and headed southeast toward the Gulf Coast instead of south to Mexico. Frank had decided to go where no one expected him to go –

even though few people knew where he was going – to elude anyone who might want to discuss the recent trouble at Big Joe's with him. For all he knew, the young man he last saw stretched out on the barroom floor was dead and his sheriff father could be investigating the crime as a swift tailwind propelled the Cessna out of Texas. Frank didn't know the young man had regained consciousness and gone looking for his girlfriend, unwilling to let his father know that some stranger had knocked him cold.

As Frank piloted the plane – its Continental engine humming reliably – toward Louisiana, he had decided on an immediate destination, another small airport where he could examine his prospects and make more definite plans. Beyond that, he recognized that his changed circumstances put New Orleans directly in his path and the long Florida peninsula not that much further away. He thought of New Orleans as a somewhat exotic place – something he would like to see – and the approaching winter gave Florida an attraction that was mainly weather-based. Mexico, he decided, would have to wait.

*

Chapter Six

Christine McKenzie – quite wealthy and more than attractive in her mid-40s – sat at a corner table in the Maritime Bar on Bourbon Street with two married friends as well as her driver, Rodney. She had stopped over in New Orleans on a return trip to south Florida, where she now lived, from Houston, another home before her late husband cashed in his eternal chips. The saloon catered to merchant mariners and bordered on sleazy, which was its principal attraction for Christine. "I like the smell of the place," she explained to those at her table, who were there only because she was. As far as they could tell, her reference was to a combination of beer, sweat and other odors that were best left undefined.

A stylish woman who had the rare ability to make herself at home almost anywhere, Chris McKenzie seemed to enjoy the noisy barroom – filled mainly with shirt-sleeved merchant sailors and sundry local drunks – and was not put off by the dense pall of cigarette smoke and the poorly made straight-up Martini she sipped on those occasions when she had forgotten how bad it was.

"I don't know what you see in this awful place," her

woman friend said, and suggested they go somewhere else before the pervading stench permeated her clothes.

"I like it here," Chris explained. It was apparent she intended to stay where she was, although the reason for that intention was a mystery to the others. They didn't realize she simply enjoyed a diversion from the tonier places she inhabited most of the time. She had explained herself when she told them she liked it where she was.

"You may like it, but I don't," the woman friend said without rancor, rising from her seat with the expectation her husband would do the same. Actually, both her husband – who seemed ambivalent about the entire matter – and Rodney stood up, although Rodney had no intention of leaving. He had been hired more as a bodyguard than a driver and had neither finished his assignment nor been paid for the work. "I'll see you for breakfast tomorrow, if you're up by then," the friend said.

"Perhaps," Chris replied as the couple left and Rodney sat down. "What now?" he asked.

Christine McKenzie acquired her substantial wealth the old fashioned way. She married a multi-millionaire, Fitzmorris, known as Fitz, McKenzie, in the days when several hundred thousand dollars was real money. The source of his wealth, he suggested, was oil, but those who knew anything about him thought it was more than likely smuggled liquor during the Prohibition years. In any event, he put the money to good use through a series of astute and reasonably legal investments that enabled him to live very well and marry an extraordinarily good looking woman 30 years his junior. He died of what a medical examiner described as "a massive coronary event triggered by over-exertion," which was another way of saying he was energetically screwing Chris when his heart gave out.

Born Christine Marie Sklodowska in North Tonawanda, New York, she was the daughter of a mill worker and his wife, who died when the girl was 10. The father was neither mean nor abusive, but he was neglectful and often drunk after his wife's death, and Christine learned early on to look after herself. She was not only pretty, but smart, particularly in practical matters, and managed with various part-time jobs during her high school years to save enough money to leave home and a father – who she never saw again – only weeks after her graduation. She went first to New York City, where she found work as a waitress in a small restaurant, and subsequently moved southwest, residing for a few years each in a couple of large cities before she moved to Houston in her early 20s. By that time and despite the onset of the Great Depression, she had learned to type at night school and found work as a receptionist for a large law firm that represented Fitz McKenzie and a host of other wealthy clients. She had also learned to dress smartly on a rigid budget and had ear-marked that particular firm and position for the sole purpose of meeting and mating with someone of substance, which she had shrewdly identified as the fastest and, perhaps, only road to riches for someone in her circumstances. Luckily for Christine, Fitz – who proposed marriage three weeks after they met – turned out a splendid husband from her point of view. At 50 when they met, he was a lean, ardent lover who took her anywhere she wanted to go and gave her almost anything she wanted. He also discovered her native intelligence and over time they came to consult on business and other important matters. And she discovered, also over time, that she loved the man she married for money and that she truly regretted his death.

Seated at the bar in the Maritime on his first night in New Orleans, Frank Bonner had watched Christine with an interest he failed to realize stemmed from her resemblance to a mature Molly Bacon, his former girlfriend. Sipping a modest scotch blend, he observed the departure of her friends and wondered about the man who remained, mainly because he sat somewhat behind her and the two rarely spoke to one another. The relationship seemed strange to Frank, particularly when he noticed the man clandestinely reach into her purse, which was slung by a strap over the back of her chair, and remove what appeared to be a large sum of money. She was completely oblivious to the loss, her attention fixed on the swarming crowd. He, meanwhile, put the bills in an interior pocket of his coat in a manner that told Frank he had just witnessed a blatant theft. "Mind your own business," he told himself, aware that anything else could lead to real trouble. At the same time, he was also drawn to this singular woman, who sat across the room from him in a state of splendid detachment from the griminess about her. "What the hell," he thought and went over to her table.

"This is none of my business," he said to Christine, who seemed to recover from a reverie, "but this man just took some money from your purse." She heard the words but failed at first to understand the meaning. Rodney, however, saw the threat to his interests and instantly stood up. A moment later he had closed the distance between himself and Frank, who found himself face to face with a barrel of a man whose face expressed considerable rage. "You want to die on the spot," Rodney said in a manner so malicious there was no doubt he meant it.

"I think you're a bloody thief," Frank replied, aware he was courting conflict, but more conscious of the situation than his antagonist because he knew when he left the bar that it would probably come to this. He had, in fact, made a perfect prediction of Rodney's reaction, and easily evaded a round-house swing that would have done damage had it landed anywhere. Unwilling to give this powerful brute a second chance, Frank dealt a crushing blow with his foot to Rodney's knee, and as he crumpled to the floor followed through with a stroke to the man's head delivered with the edges of his two hands clasp together. Rodney broke a chair and a couple of ribs on his way down and came to rest on his back with the lapels of his jacket folded outward. Frank leaned over his unconscious body and retrieved the money, which he handed to Christine. "I believe this is yours," he said.

"Who in hell are you," she replied.

"Nobody you know," was his response before he went on to explain what he had seen and why he had intervened. "I hate a thief," he added.

"I hate a crooked bodyguard," she said, rising slowly from her seat and collecting the hand bag into which she stuffed the money. And while his brief scuffle with Rodney had not attracted a great deal of attention in a place where fights were common enough, Frank noticed that several men in the area seemed interested in Christine's cash. "I'd like to see you safely out of here," he offered. "No strings attached."

She smiled an acceptance and they left the Maritime Bar, but not before Frank casually adjusted the front of his jacket to reveal a holstered pistol for the benefit of anyone with more than idle curiosity about Christine's money. The combination of the gun and his work on Rodney – who had regained consciousness but was still too dazed to care – allowed the couple to leave the place unmolested. “Where to?” Frank inquired.

“I could stand a decent drink,” Christine suggested, and he recommended the bar in his hotel, which was just off Canal Street and only a few blocks away.

“I forgot to pay for my drink at the Maritime,” Frank told her 15 minutes later when they had found a small table and been seated in a corner of the hotel bar.

“And you broke one of their chairs with Rodney,” she pointed out, “but that's just the cost of doing business in a place like that.” Christine went on to explain that Rodney had been hired on the recommendation of a friend's associate to see her safely back to Florida from a business trip to Houston. She had meant to put the money – which was only a couple of thousand dollars – in some safe place, but had forgotten in her haste to meet the friends who had left her at the Maritime. Rodney, she speculated, had probably noticed the cash when she opened her purse to retrieve something else. “And now,” she continued, “what about you?” She wondered particularly about where he had learned to fight and why he carried a gun, but settled for what he was willing to tell her. His general conduct and manner had gained her confidence and she was willing to give him the benefit of any doubts she might have.

“There's not much to tell,” he began, and then told her he was an ex-Marine who had recently attended a university and run a small business with a friend, who had gone off to fight North Koreans. He also told her about the Cessna – which was parked – safely, he hoped – at a small airport some 30 miles from the city. He didn't tell her about the fight at Big Joe's or about his other recent bouts, which he preferred to forget. "I'm a reasonably peaceful, mostly honest man," he concluded, "who sometimes carries a gun because it's a dangerous world out there."

"Fair enough," she said.

They had a couple of leisurely drinks and talked for several hours before Chris took the initiative and suggested they go to his room in the hotel. "I'm old enough to be your mother, but I'm willing to overlook that little impediment to romance if you are," she said.

"I can manage that," he assured her and paid the bar bill.

In his room somewhat later, Frank made a confession. "I haven't had much experience at this," he told Chris as his hand wandered gently over her incredibly smooth body, the product of exercise and very expensive emollients.

"Then, it's time you got some," she replied and began to show him what she thought he had missed, modestly unaware the experience wouldn't have been the same without her. Frank had been attracted to Chris from the moment he saw her in the Maritime, although he would not have defined his feelings as love. Given his nature, he would not have defined his feelings at all. She, too, felt the attraction without the need to categorize it. Fitz McKenzie had been her lover and father figure, all rolled into one, and he would retain those positions for the rest of her life.

Still later, they lay naked on their backs next to each other, neither of them surprised the union had gone so well. They had earlier talked themselves into a form of compatibility that almost guaranteed the physical part would succeed, assuming their essential organs were in working order. "Would you like to work for me?" she asked after a while. "I need someone to look after my interests and I don't want another goon."

"Are you offering me a job as your bodyguard?" He was amused by the job title and his nearness at that moment to the object he would be guarding.

"You could call it that," she responded seductively, and provided a wordless summons to do again what they had done before. "Anything worth doing is worth doing twice," he observed and they did it.

Afterward, Frank told her he wasn't looking for work – particularly the kind that made him subordinate to anyone – but he didn't have any immediate plans and would like to spend the approaching winter near her in a warm climate. "You don't have to pay me to protect your splendid body," he said. "I should pay you for the privilege."

"Are you calling me a whore?" she replied with a wry smile.

Frank gave the matter some thought and then kissed her. "If I am," he said at last, "it's only because you're my kind of whore."

They spent the night in Frank's room and had breakfast there the next morning before he checked out of the hotel. Together, they took a taxi to the home of her married friends, the couple he had seen but not met the prior evening in the Maritime Bar. Chris had originally planned to spend the night with them, but they were not surprised when she didn't. They had learned early in their relationship that her behavior was hard to predict, and they knew she had been accompanied by a sturdy bodyguard. "Where's Rodney?' the woman asked when she answered the doorbell and saw Chris and Frank, who carried his small, canvas traveling bag.

"That's a long and boring story," Chris replied, "but I

can shorten it if you've got some coffee." She then introduced Frank to the woman, whose name was Fran, and to the husband, Burt, who soon joined them before they sought out a table set on old cobblestones at the back of their rambling house. The area was densely but carefully vegetated, which gave it an aura of serene privacy and old money.

"Tell me what happened and where you found this good looking young man?" Fran asked as they sat down. Some minutes later a maid would appear with coffee and small pastries. Meanwhile, Frank listened as Chris told them about Rodney's behavior, and her revised plan to fly home - her home – with him. "He has a small plane and a hankering to go south for the winter," she said.

"What kind of plane?" Burt inquired of Frank, who answered the question before the two men lapsed again into silence, and Chris asked if there was some way to deliver her car and the bulk of her traveling clothes to Florida. She understood the Cessna was too small for heavy luggage and that it would not be difficult to find someone who was both reliable and interested in driving her Bentley on a road trip. "I'll take care of it," Burt offered, and later drove them to the airport, partly as a simple courtesy but also to see Frank's plane. His curiosity about the Cessna was prompted solely by his concern for Chris' safety, although he knew she would make the flight with or without his approval.

"Where did you meet them?" Frank later asked Chris about her friends as they cruised in fair weather along the Gulf coast. He understood the limitations of his experience as well as the plane's instrumentation and had no intention of taking a more direct course across open water.

"Burt and my husband were old friends." she explained. "They were both friends and occasional business partners long before I met Fitz." She answered his question but her attention was partially diverted to the broad expanse of water off to her right and to the terrain below that seemed to pass in slow motion as the 120 flew east past Biloxi and Mobile into the Florida panhandle.

"What kind of business?" He felt some obligation to conduct a conversation even though his attention, too, was divided by the need to pilot the aircraft. It was not difficult, however, to maintain a true heading, given the compass on his instrument panel and the Gulf of Mexico which, he noted, was where it should be.

"I don't really know," Chris said. "Someone once told me Burt made his original money running guns to various political and military factions in Latin America, but that's only hearsay."

"I had the impression he'd inherited his money," Frank observed.

Chris explained that Burt did come from an old, once-wealthy family – from Baltimore, she thought – that had fallen on hard times. But he, Burt, had probably resurrected his fortunes through murky deals that earned him enough money to reassume the trappings of respectability. She told him Burt still had connections that were useful when she had to get "certain things" done.

"Things?"

"All kinds of things," she explained, "everything from hiring a thug like Rodney to major investment transactions." Frank had originally categorized Burt as a pleasant but pampered socialite who had probably never done an honest day's work in his life. He was now beginning to realize he was only right about the honest day's work. The turn-around in his impression of Burt was complete when she told him the beating he gave Rodney was only a prelude to something far worse. "Burt's a gentleman, in his way, but you don't want to cross him," she said.

"Neat," Frank thought, but restrained that particular comment. He was trying to cultivate a more sophisticated image than the word would have conveyed. "He's an interesting chap," he remarked instead.

Frank was pleasantly surprised to find good weather clear into northern Florida where they stopped for the night at a small coastal airport near a resort that was far from fancy but still provided better than average accommodations - available because the winter season was yet to begin – and a restaurant that was mostly devoid of patrons at that time of the year. Seated on a broad, open porch where a soft but steady breeze brought in the unmistakable smell of salt water, the two were pleased to escape the monotonous drone of the Cessna's engine. "I like your little airplane," Chris said, lingering over her second Martini as they awaited dinner service, "but let's take my plane next time. It's larger and faster."

"You've got a plane?" he replied, thinking at first she was merely kidding him about the 120's size.

"I've got a twin Beech parked at the airport near my home, and access to a couple of ex-military pilots who seem to know what they're doing," she said. He quickly realized she was serious and apparently owned a Beechcraft Model 18, a twin engine plane that could haul anywhere from six to 11 passengers and had seen wide service during the Second World War with both the

U.S. Army Air Force and the Navy. "You probably feel like you're slumming," he observed, making a comparison between his modest little airplane and hers.

"I think the Cessna is cute," she said. "It's just a bit small and, perhaps, a tad slow for trips to anywhere other than the grocery store."

"When was the last time you went to the grocery store?" He was beginning to suspect the extent of her wealth was a good deal greater than his original assumption. He knew she was comfortably situated, but he also knew that even the reasonably affluent didn't usually own their own twin engine planes with access to professional flight crews. "Just how wealthy are you?" he asked with his usual candor.

"I've got a ton of money, left to me by a sweet, generous husband," Chris responded. "I tell you that because I don't think it's my money you're after."

"You've got that right," he said, reaching across the table to touch her hand as a young waitress delivered the first course in their meal. Chris would never realize her feelings for Frank were a mixture, perhaps uneven, of the romantic and maternal. She was old enough to be his mother and had, even then, certain protective impulses toward him, although there was an even stronger physical attraction she knew was reciprocal. Her feelings – which, like Frank, she didn't bother to examine too closely – verged on the incestuous. His situation, meanwhile, was far less complicated. He was a young man who had been strongly attracted to a fine looking older woman who bore no resemblance to his mother.

They made love that night and again early in the morning – as new lovers often do – but still arose before sunrise to ensure the last leg of their flight could be made in the shortened hours that marked the approach of winter. They were also traveling in the hurricane season, but their luck held and they made the rest of the trip in near perfect flying weather with several stops along the way. They arrived in mid-afternoon at the airport where her plane was based, another small field but this one equipped to handle the privately-owned planes that ferried wealthy owners to Florida when the northern weather turned cold. As Frank taxied in from the paved runway, she directed him to the hangar – one of several not far from a stucco terminal building – where her plane was kept. There was someone in that hangar who would find a suitable place to put his plane, she explained, and then drive them to her home. She had phoned ahead the previous evening and made those arrangements.

"Your home," he asked as he switched off the engine in response to an attendant who had motioned them to a parking spot, "is it a palace or a castle?"

"Just a humble cottage," she said, and he soon discovered the limited extent of her humility. Although not large by standards of the very wealthy and less than a half hour drive from the airport, it was perfectly sited on a broad stretch of private beach and barely detectable on its other sides as the result of its distance from the road and a long, white wall, broken only by a heavy metal gate that provided entry to the property. The interior of the house, Frank soon discovered, was distinguished not by its expanse of terrazzo floors or its succession of large, sparsely furnished rooms, but by the significant number of paintings and other forms of art that clung to its walls. "I like pictures," she explained when he first saw the place.

At the time, Frank was unfamiliar with the more

prominent artists, mostly Mexicans, who had done some of the work, among them Diego Rivera, David Siqueiros, Jose Orozco and Raphael Tomayo. He would learn about those and others like them in the months ahead as she sought to inform him about something that had considerable importance for her.

The size of the house was determined more by its length than its width, a reality Frank noticed when he passed through the front door and saw, across the narrow room, the Gulf of Mexico beyond a bank of tall windows that dominated the wall. He had barely digested the view when a small, middle-aged woman – her black hair pulled back and knotted – arrived from some interior place in the house. "Welcome home," she greeted Chris, who rushed over to warmly embrace this servant who, Frank surmised, was more than a mere domestic.

"Angelina, this is Frank," Chris said. "He'll be staying with us for a while." The woman – who derived from one of the Central American countries – examined him with a maternal eye. She had not yet decided on his worth, but disguised that indecision with absolute discretion. "Welcome to you, too," she added. He soon learned that Angelina and her husband, Jorge, had worked for Chris since the early days of her marriage. They now ran the house and supervised the various individuals and contractors who were hired to maintain and repair everything from the extensively landscaped grounds to the mechanical and other needs inside the residence. Only a few years older than Chris, they never-the-less treated her like the daughter they never had while she regarded them in personal matters like members of her extended family.

"This house has been a tomb without you," Jorge said

to Chris after he had introduced himself to Frank and placed two straight-up Martinis, perfectly chilled, on the small table between the lounge chairs where they had settled somewhat earlier to watch one of those famous Gulf coast sunsets. Easily as discrete as his wife, Jorge then quickly and quietly left them on the small terrace above the beach to continue their discussion about Frank's role in the household. She had seen him dispatch Rodney in the Maritime Bar and realized from his general behavior he could probably be trusted to not only protect her person but her interests as well. She soon understood that he, too, had a practical smartness that might complement their relationship in a number of ways.

As the sun slowly descended behind the Gulf and a soft wind rustled through nearby palm fronds, Frank disclosed the arrangement he had conceived. "I'd like to get an aircraft instrument rating and learn to fly something with more than a single engine," he explained. "If you'll make the twin Beech available to me, I'll hang around as anything from a bodyguard to a personal assistant with bedroom privileges." He thought for a moment and added: "I'll even pay your first pilot for the instruction time."

She bought the proposal immediately, but took a leisurely sip of her drink to suggest the matter required some thought. "I can live with that," she said after a while and suggested he take up residence in one of the many spare bedrooms in the house, preferably one not far from hers. "And I can live with that," he agreed.

Over the following weeks and as winter descended on the northern states, Frank and Chris settled into a routine that served both their purposes. He learned to watch over her without intruding on the personal space she valued and to assist in certain business matters that required judgment rather than specialized training and experience. At the same time, he took instructions from her chief pilot, Grady Bracken, a veteran of the recent war who had flown cargo planes over "The Hump" in a dangerous, high altitude military supply route that crossed parts of India and Burma into southwestern China early in the effort when navigational equipment and weather forecasts were as primitive as the aircraft. Still earlier and before the war broke out, he had barnstormed in a beat-up bi-plane around the Midwest.

"I'd say small world if I hadn't flown over so much of it," Bracken said to Frank as they flew the Beechcraft southeast toward Miami. He referred to the minor revelation that he knew Bill Hager, who owned the small airport in Illinois where Frank learned to fly. Frank had mentioned Hager in reference to something he soon forgot, and Bracken revealed that their paths had crossed on a number of occasions back in their barnstorming days. "I didn't expect he'd still be alive," the pilot observed. "He's crashed more planes than I've flown."

Frank could tell that the recollection of Hager and old times had jogged something in Bracken's memory. Normally restrained to the point of speechlessness, the veteran pilot became almost conversational as he recalled incidents – mostly concerned with near fatal plane crashes – that involved Hager and others he had known. But the stories, Frank soon discovered, were more than mere anecdotes. Bracken had neatly arranged the various incidents to make a number of salient points, mostly about flying in bad or marginal weather and other follies that were likely to shorten a pilot's life. Frank got the message, given his earlier bad weather experiences in both the Stearman and the Cessna. Bracken, he understood, was providing him with the mantra to long life as a pilot.

Strapped into a seat in the passenger compartment, Chris was fast asleep when they landed at the Miami airport and taxied to a fixed base operation where the plane could be fueled and parked during their weekend in the area. She had dozed off with a stack of papers on her lap, material related to a real estate transaction that was justification for the trip.

"Interesting stuff," Frank observed as he gently nudged her awake, and then collected their overnight bags from the back of the cabin. Bracken had already left the plane to register their arrival at a small nearby office and to make arrangements for transportation to a Miami Beach hotel.

"I hate this tacky place," Chris remarked as she gathered the papers together and unbuckled her seatbelt.

"Why buy property here if you hate it so much?" Frank asked as they emerged from the plane into brilliant sunlight.

"Greed," she replied, searching her purse for a pair of sunglasses. "Pure greed." She went on to explain she owned the property and that it wasn't anywhere near Miami but the prospective buyer was. He was beginning to realize that Chris was far more than a wealthy widow. Her dead husband may have founded the family fortune, but she had not only maintained but expanded it through shrewd, sometimes audacious, deals that often surprised the experienced, sometimes rapacious, people she outwitted. Her formal education had ended with high school, but Fitz McKenzie had taught her things they didn't teach at Harvard's graduate school of business. And her good looks often diverted attention from that knowledge and her general intelligence, particularly when she dealt with over-confident men who lived with the presumption of success.

Later that afternoon, Bracken drove them in a rental car to the hotel, where they registered and then went on to a large, private home off a rather busy waterway. Here, they were greeted by the resident, Henry Trippa, a heavyset man in a flowery, short-sleeved shirt, white shorts and sandals who led them – with the exception of Bracken, who remained with the car – to a back yard dock and his 52 foot Chris-craft motor yacht. Once aboard and seated in the main salon, Chris introduced the two men. “What do you do?” Trippa inquired.

“This and that,” Frank replied.

They were soon joined by another man, somewhat younger than Trippa with a bull neck and barely enough forehead to separate his eyebrows from his hairline. The newcomer wore a white linen jacket that seemed a little small for his robust frame. “This is my business associate, Mr. Hartley,” Trippa said and motioned him to have a seat, which he wordlessly did.

“Business associate, my ass,” Frank thought. He had little experience with people of this sort, but he knew a goon when he saw one. Somewhat more experienced but not particularly concerned, Christine recognized Hartley for the thug he was, but had other matters on her mind. She soon got down to business, a discussion about the sale of a vast parcel of undeveloped land in the southwestern part of the state where a large, regional airport would, rumor had it, eventually be constructed. There were political forces at work even then to make the airport a reality and greatly increase the value of that land, she told Trippa. They both knew the land was mostly inaccessible and otherwise worthless, but a decision to build the airport would alter that reality and provide the speculative opportunity of a lifetime. The thousands of acres Christine owned were sufficient to accommodate the airport and the community that would grow up around it.

"What about the nature freaks?" Trippa asked.

"There is a small group of environmentalists who oppose the project," Chris admitted. "They think construction of an airport in that area would reduce the flow of water into the southern wetlands." She went on to tell him their opposition was manageable, given the substantial economic benefits a project of that size would bring to an economically depressed part of the state. She didn't tell him, however, that essential federal funds for the project were unlikely at that time as a result of the expense of waging war on the Korean Peninsula. She also didn't tell him the rumors about the airport were based mainly on conjecture, wishful thinking and misinformation, which Chris herself had spread to promote the sale of her property.

"I'll think about it," Trippa said after further discussion and cursory examination of maps and legal documents which he would turn over to his attorney and others for their opinions about the proposed deal. "I also think you're asking a lot of money for that scrubby wilderness."

"There's no particular rush," Chris assured him and then carefully revoked that assurance by telling him there were others interested in the land. "That scrubby wilderness might one day make the price I'm asking look like small change," she added.

Frank and Hartley, meanwhile, took the measure of one another, mostly because they were excluded from the discussion and there was little else for them to do. Neither of these men feared the other, although Frank had his usual advantage. He had gauged Hartley's considerable strength and understood that he probably employed it from time to time in unsavory ways. Hartley, however, had no notion of Frank's martial abilities or his connection to the woman who dealt with his boss on equal terms. He knew nothing about Frank and cared even less.

"How well do you know this character?" Frank, referring to Henry Trippa, asked Chris as they were driven back to the hotel.

"Not well at all," she replied. "Why do you ask?"

"He seems a little shady to me," Frank said.

"He's more than a little shady," Chris admitted. "He's a crook in every sense of the word, but he's got the kind of money it takes to do this deal."

Frank wondered about the wisdom of doing speculative business with someone who has underworld connections – someone who probably expects a sure thing and keeps Mr. Hartley around for those occasions when his expectations are disappointed – but he correctly assumed Chris was aware of the risk. She later told him that her friend, Burt, had put her in touch with Trippa. "My friendship with Burt is the ultimate insurance policy," she explained. "Nobody screws with Burt or his friends."

"I'm developing more respect for Burt all the time," Frank said, but he had serious reservations about her dealings with Trippa. He was beginning to understand she was in this rather dangerous game as much for the game itself as for the money. She was easily smart enough to understand the risk, he knew, but she breezed fearlessly through the meeting and was completely at ease during the ride back to the hotel. "I'm more than ready for a drink," she announced as Bracken steered the rental car up to the typically extravagant entrance to the beach hotel. The weather had turned a bit chilly and a light rain had begun to fall as he deposited them at the entrance and drove off to spend the night, he told them, with an "old Air Force friend" who lived on the other side of Biscayne Bay.

"Air Force friend, indeed," Chris said somewhat later in their small suite when she had settled comfortably on the bed in her flimsy undergarments with one of two Martinis Frank mixed before he went into the adjoining room to phone Nick Satterfield in St. Louis. "I'll give you eight to five odds – and God bless him – that he's got some bimbo lined up across town." She spoke as Frank returned, holding his glass by its long, slender stem, and sat on the bed next to her. The expression on his face was more serious, she thought, than the occasion warranted. "Something wrong?" she asked.

"My friend, Jack Smiley, has gone missing in Korea," he said softly, and then took a sip from his drink before he kissed her gently on the lips.

*

Chapter Seven

Jack Smiley went missing in action with the 1st Marine Division some time during the 10 days that some 30,000 United Nations troops in Korea fought four times that number of Chinese in the Battle of Chosin Reservoir, a deadly engagement made even worse by the frigid weather conditions and rugged terrain. Jack had been called to active duty on a warm day in mid-August and by late November found himself in a frozen nightmare made possible by General Douglas MacArthur's refusal to believe the Chinese would enter the war if he chased the essentially defeated North Korean army to the Yalu River on China's border. It was a colossal blunder on the General's part that would have been even worse had the United Nations forces not been able to fight their way out of encirclement and other dilemmas at substantial cost to both themselves and the Chinese, who sustained heavy losses during this bitter campaign.

At the time, the war itself was less than six months old, beginning on June 25, 1950 when North Korean troops crossed the 38th parallel into South Korea. The invasion provided justification for United Nations military involvement and only days later president Harry Truman authorized U.S. air force and navy support of South Korea followed by a commitment of ground troops. In July, Douglas MacArthur was put in command of all UN forces.

Only a month before the Chinese communists poured in their numbers across the Yalu River, the war seemed all but over and Jack had written Frank Bonner a letter suggesting he might be home early in the following year. He thought he might return to the university and wondered if they might pool their funds – money made from sale of The Outpost – in some new business arrangement that would make them happy and wealthy before they were prone to male pattern baldness. Frank read the short letter only once, folded it neatly and put it into a compartment of his wallet. Other than his announcement to Chris, he never mentioned the loss of his friend to anyone else, but the event had a major influence on the way he saw life in general. He was made more aware that almost everyone – even those with great wealth and power – have very little control over the forces that govern their lives. "Heads of state and the poor alike are afflicted with inoperable brain tumors and other calamities," he thought, "so don't worry about that kind of stuff. Put your efforts into controlling only those things that are controllable and screw the rest." This realization was not so profound it eluded everyone else, but Frank thought about its practical applications and focused his energies on things he knew were possible and useful. At the same time, he also discarded those things that were of minor importance. "It's not a brain tumor," he usually told those who came to him with trivial complaints.

"I understand Henry Trippa isn't very happy with the land you sold him," Frank told Christine more than a year after the deal had been made and when prospects for the new airport had all but vanished. Frank got the information from Burt, who had learned to trust him as he became more of a fixture in Christine's business and personal life.

"Henry who?" She had not forgotten the man or the transaction, but saw no reason to ponder the past. She had made a substantial profit from sale of that land and had long since gone on to other things. But Frank was not so sanguine about the matter.

"I know you're not concerned about Trippa, but I am," Frank said. "He's not likely to forget what you did to him, and I suspect he's the kind who likes to get more than even."

"That's why I have you and Burt to protect me," she replied, seated next to him in the first class section of a commercial flight to their immediate destination, Mexico City. They planned later to go on to Taxco in the mountains and then Acapulco on the Pacific coast for a long-delayed vacation. Meanwhile, Burt had promised Frank to use his connections to find out if Trippa posed any threat to Christine. "If there is, let me know what I can do," Frank had suggested, although he thought, correctly, that Burt figured he was too inexperienced to handle someone like Trippa. Frank respected the older man's reservations, and made no effort to convince him otherwise. Instead, he – like Christine – relied on Burt for the information and advice he could provide from an incredible variety of sources, and the sure knowledge he could do what had to be done on his own initiative if the need arose. He also knew he was Christine's first line of defense, given his physical nearness to her in every respect.

As the airliner's four reciprocating engines filled the cabin with a steady drone, Frank at first tried, once again, to alert Chris to the Trippa threat, but soon recognized the futility of his effort. She calculated that Burt's reputation would protect her, as it had before, and was not inclined to needlessly worry about something she considered beyond her control. "I've put you in my will," she said, partly as a conversational diversion but also to tell him something about the position he had assumed in her life.

"You've what?"

"You heard me," she replied and went on to explain that he, Angelina and Jorge were included in a new will she had drawn only days earlier. She didn't tell him the bulk of her estate would go to him, although the other two would get more than enough to sustain them in comfort for the rest of their lives.

"I appreciate the thought, but I don't need your money," he informed her.

"If you did, you probably wouldn't get it," she explained, pointing out that his independence had told her their relationship was based on more than money. She had long since come to realize his attraction to her was genuine, as was his regard for her safety and comfort. "I love you, Frankie," she said, using the diminutive of his name for the first time, partly in fun. She knew, too, that he was not good at professions of affection and was surprised at his response.

"I love you, too," he said and quickly changed the subject. He also quickly forgot her announcement about the will, assuming she would – despite the difference in their ages – outlive him. It was a subject they never again discussed, although the gesture on her part showed the distance their relationship had traveled in little more than a year.

Somewhat later when they had put aside reading materials and resumed a conversation, Frank told her he had sold the Cessna. The continued instruction from Bracken and ground school courses had not only given him proficiency with the Beechcraft but the licenses he needed to legally pilot the more sophisticated airplane.

"I'm putting the cash from sale of the plane along with a few thousand more into Burt's little Costa Rican deal," he explained. She wasn't familiar with that particular enterprise, but let the matter pass because she knew Burt invariably had a number of things going on at the same time. "You and Burt have gotten to be real pals," she said instead.

"We have a mutual interest," he remarked. That mutual interest, of course, was Christine, but Burt had gradually developed not only respect but a degree of fondness for Frank, whose handling of Rodney in the Maritime Bar gained, once he learned of it, his instant approval. Burt would have handled the situation in essentially the same way, only with a difference. He would have hired someone else to thrash Rodney, which he later did and which accounted for the former body guard's permanent limp and his move to a remote part of the country. He had paid dearly for the piddling amount of cash extracted from Christine's purse.

"I like Burt, but he has some peculiar notions," Frank observed, basing the opinion on a variety of eccentricities the older man had revealed in the course of dozens of phone conversations the two men had conducted in the months they had known each other.

"You have no idea," Chris said with absolute assurance about a man she had known well for a long time. “Under that patrician veneer beats the heart of a marauding barbarian.” Frank had a hard time visualizing Burt in that way, but he was beginning to realize the man’s overtly civilized manner was not necessarily the whole story. “Any chance I’ll develop some insight into his dark interior when we get together in Acapulco?” he inquired. They were scheduled to meet Burt and his wife, Fran, and spend several days together at one of the cliff-top hotels toward the end of the trip.

“I have no doubt you’ll see a side of Burt that wasn’t apparent in the phone calls you two exchanged,” she ventured and then dropped the subject, unwilling to unravel her friend’s mysterious nature behind his back. Frank and Burt had mainly discussed Christine’s business affairs as the younger man gradually assumed a more important role in those matters as well as her personal life. At the same time, Frank was achieving a degree of commercial sophistication not generally available to those his age as well as the respect of the older man, who had recently paid him, he thought, something of a compliment. “I was pleased to learn you’re more than a nice looking chap with a big dick,” Burt said at the conclusion of one of their phone calls.

Later, Frank was surprised by the compact elegance of the hotel Chris had selected, a relatively small building with a discrete entrance and a second floor lobby devoid of random foot traffic. Their suite, however, was large by any standard and the room service – which provided them with cocktails after they had settled in - was, in Christine’s words, “pleasantly prompt.” She allowed that her appreciation may have been the result of thirst brought on by a long commercial flight which, she further admitted, was preferable to an even longer trip had they made it in the Beechcraft. “I know you like to fly that damned thing," she said, "but the airline got us here faster and we had an opportunity to talk a bit along the way."

They lay on their backs – quite naked again and side by side – in the middle of the vast bed, too far from the end tables where they would otherwise have put their drinks. Instead, he rested the bottom of his glass on the sheets and she used his chest as an improvised platform. "Is that too chilly?" she inquired, avoiding the word "cold" in an effort to minimize its impact.

They had elected to stay in the suite that evening in deference to Mexico City's significant altitude – more than 7,000 feet – which required some physical adjustment for those who had recently traveled from the lowlands. But Christine had scheduled a busy series of activities that would begin the following day with a tour of the archaeological park at Teotihuacan some 30 miles northeast of Mexico City. She only revealed these plans after they achieved mutual satisfaction, which pretty much guaranteed his acceptance of the idea. "Anything you say," he said, barely aware of the schedule she had set for him as he put an arm around her bare shoulders and went to sleep.

"They don't seem to know much about this place," Frank observed to Chris as they stood together the next day atop the Pyramid of the Sun, a massive structure they had laboriously climbed after a tour guide told them what little he knew about Teotihuacan.

"They know enough for now," she replied, and reminded him the guide had actually provided a good deal of information. The place had once been the largest city in the Americas and during its heyday around 500 AD was larger than Rome. The pyramid on which they stood was the third largest in the world and, while the origins were uncertain, construction in the area probably began in the first two centuries before Christ and its civilization reached its zenith somewhere between 350 and 650 AD. Some think the inhabitants immigrated to the place from the Valley of Mexico to the south, possibly refugees from a volcanic eruption, the guide had told them.

"It's interesting," Frank admitted, "but it's still mainly a mystery. Who were they, where did they come from and where did they go?"

"Ah," she replied, "but it's the search for answers – more than the answers – that's interesting."

"There are some things that don't have answers," Frank said. "Most people aren't willing to accept that reality, which explains their need for religion. It's a device that provides answers, even though those answers were invented by men from whole cloth. Personally, I can live with the knowledge there are things I'll never know. That knowledge allows me to sleep well at night and, especially, on Sunday mornings."

She had not previously discussed religion with Frank, but his attitude – not entirely different from her own agnostic tendencies – came as no great surprise. "It's ironic," she replied, "that I've brought an atheist to a place where religious belief was strong enough to justify human sacrifice." She thought for a moment and then added: "I'm willing to forgive your lack of faith, but only because you're cute." She knew he knew he was a lot of things, none of them cute. He also knew she liked to yank his chain, which was alright with him if it gave her pleasure.

Chris recognized that Frank was more interested in the historical rather than the archeological past, and the next day took him to Chapultepec Park in Mexico City where U.S. Marines had stormed a hill during the Mexican-American War in 1847. "The red stripe on the pants of the Marine Corps dress uniform symbolizes the bloody battle of Chapultepec heights," he told her. He didn't tell her the stripe honors all fallen marines, particularly the non-commissioned officers who sustained the heaviest casualties on the American side in that battle. He also didn't tell her – because he didn't know at the time – that those marines charged the hill into withering gunfire delivered by six Mexican military cadets, ages 14 to 20, who died in the fighting. An old palace on that hill had been turned into a military academy in 1833, which accounted for the presence of the cadets.

"I took you to the park today, and tomorrow you're going to take me to school," she told him that evening at dinner.

"It's the least I can do," he replied, completely unaware of what she had in mind, but confident it had nothing to do with climbing another pyramid. Actually, she had enrolled them for a one-day lecture on the country's history, delivered in English at the University of Mexico. Frank, she learned, had been intrigued by the Spanish conquest of an Aztec empire – carried out by a small but ruthless collection of armor-plated misfits – and she wanted him to know there was more to the place than that one compelling episode. He had suspected as much, but had not yet taken time to confirm the suspicion. This single lecture, however, initiated a process for Frank that would evolve into one of his paramount interests, the study of Mexican history at first and later a more generalized approach to the subject. He would eventually understand he had the process backward – since increasing specialization was generally the more accepted course - but he was not a professional historian and wasn't bound by that convention. And while the Spanish conquest of Mexico remained for him both a lesson in dogged determination as well as an incredible and unlikely adventure, he would gradually extend his interest from the earliest recorded events to periods that verged on his own lifetime.

The man most responsible for Frank's historical epiphany was George Kerensky, an American of Russian descent from somewhere in New Jersey who conducted the lecture that day, and afterward engaged them in conversation. Frank was aware from the beginning that Kerensky – a small, intense man with dark, unruly hair – was attracted to Christine, who was amused rather than flattered by the attention, and who soon found a way to employ that attraction to a useful purpose. They had found a knowledgeable and willing guide to Mexico City.

"I arrived here 10 years ago, about the time they assassinated Leon Trotsky," Kerensky told them. His reference was to the murder of one of the principal revolutionaries who founded the Soviet Union and who was expelled from Russia in 1929 for relentless criticism of the direction Joseph Stalin had taken the country. One of Stalin's agents had penetrated Trotsky's heavily guarded house near Mexico City and planted a small ice axe in his skull with predictable results. "It was an interesting time, just after the Spanish civil war in the 1930s when many Mexican volunteers had fought the Fascists, and just before the outbreak of the Second World War," he added.

Frank soon figured out that Kerensky had spent the entire war in Mexico, which led him to wonder if the evasion of military service had been the main reason he settled in the country. "No matter," he concluded. "The little bastard is one hell of a lecturer and probably knows more about Mexican history than the president of Mexico." With that thought in mind, he tolerated Kerensky's lascivious notions about Chris, confident he was a worthy tour guide and that she would rather cut off an arm than have anything amorous to do with him.

"I'll show you Trotsky's house and Diego Rivera painting a mural," he told them and delivered on both counts. The Trotsky house was in Coyoacan – which in 1940 had been on the outskirts of the city – and Rivera at work was only a stone's throw from the classroom where Kerensky had delivered his lecture. The painter – when they saw him from a distance – was halfway up a wall on a scaffold, producing yet another large vision of revolutionary triumph. He had at one time been Trotsky's friend, but the two men had fallen out some time before Stalin managed to strike down his old enemy.

"These Mexican artists are for the most part political animals," Kerensky explained, using David Siqueiros as another example. Siqueiros – who with Rivera and Jose Orozco were not only famous in their own country but had international reputations as well – was implicated in an unsuccessful attempt on Trotsky's life not long before he was successfully assassinated. The painter was accused along with other Stalinists of invading Trotsky's house to the inner courtyard, where they set up machine guns and peppered the place with bullets but failed, miraculously, to kill anyone. Siqueiros was later jailed and subsequently exiled, which became something of a pattern in his tempestuous life.

Frank listened to Kerensky's stories about the artists and made the connection with some of the paintings that hung in Christine's house. The pictures were not murals, of course, but the works had been rendered by the same hands that had produced, he soon realized, what some considered masterpieces of a particular kind. This realization made him anxious to examine more closely the paintings that Chris prized and he had previously taken for granted. "You're beginning to get it," she told him when he expressed that interest.

"Maybe," he replied.

Several days later, Frank had declined a breakfast invitation from Kerensky that would have interfered with his morning work-out, a grueling routine he had developed over the years and one he usually carried out in seclusion at least four days a week and sometimes five. He and Chris often awoke before sunrise to make love, and she invariably went back to sleep while he went off to do the work-out he felt compelled to do. She sometimes wondered where he got the energy that enabled him to build a degree of strength she had not seen in anyone else. She admired his discipline, but it was only one of a number of qualities that attracted her to him.

"The little creep made a pass at me," Christine, who had accepted Kerensky's breakfast invitation, told Frank when she returned to the hotel.

"What happened?" he asked with some confidence she had not been deflowered.

"He slapped me on my bottom, and I knocked him on his equivalent part," she said with absolute accuracy. She had landed a round house punch that laid Kerensky flat on his back. Surprisingly, however, the set-back had neither embarrassed nor discouraged him . He had risen from the sidewalk and followed her down the street asking her pardon until she managed to hail a taxi and leave him standing alone with no remorse.

Later that day, Kerensky phoned an apology to Chris, which she accepted with one provision. "If you do that or anything like it again, your teeth go next," she said. Frank overheard the conversation, and afterward gave her his own take on the situation. "I'm beginning to feel sorry for the horny, little shit," he observed.

Reinstated as their guide and even more attracted to her as a result of the incident, Kerensky over the next few days took them to an assortment of tourist attractions ranging from the floating gardens of Xochimilco to a performance that was billed as a burlesque show but featured Perez Prado and his famous Mombo band and a large-breasted woman – covered from neck to ankles in an emerald green gown – who walked up and down the stage in profile while the largely male audience lost its collective head in passionate response. "Am I missing something?" Frank whispered to Christine, who was equally confused by the reaction.

"This is a rather constrained society, at least on the surface," Kerensky explained. "Below the surface is quite a different matter."

Kerensky's diagnosis of Mexican society may or may not have been accurate, but Christine had no doubt their diminutive guide was not to be trusted where women were concerned. "He's the sneakiest little twit I've ever met," she told Frank when they had returned to the hotel.

"Has he bothered you again?"

"Not overtly," she explained. "I doubt he'd put his hands on me after our recent episode, but he has yet to look me directly in the eyes. He's constantly ogling my breasts or anything else I keep reasonably covered from polite society."

“Do you want me to have a chat with Mr. Kerensky?” Frank offered. He explained he meant only a discussion and nothing more. “The man is more of a challenge to himself than anyone else,” he said. In this case, Frank had seriously misjudged his subject. Kerensky, true enough, was no physical challenge to most other men, but he had earned a living off older, wealthy women, many of them widowed or divorced and most on vacation from the United States. He had broken no laws, but had damaged a number of aging hearts through his predatory conduct and absolute disregard for anyone’s feelings but his own. He had not stolen anything from these women, but had accepted expensive gifts and money as well as their willingness to take him to fine restaurants and other places he would otherwise not been able to afford.

Neither Frank nor Christine would have thought Kerensky capable of attracting – let alone seducing – the number of women he had accumulated, but they also would not have taken into account the toll loneliness can extract from those susceptible to the condition. Kerensky, however, had a keen eye for this vulnerability, and used it to supplement his modest earnings as a university instructor whose work brought him into regular contact with lonely female tourists.

Although Kerensky was quite good at making those connections, he was equally bad in his frequent efforts to bed strong-willed, attractive women of any age. But he was not easily discouraged, as Chris discovered when he began to suggest with increasing frequency that they have a sexual relationship. He did it with such subtlety, however, she found it difficult to confront him with the warning she knew he deserved. She knew he would simply deny her accusation. Meanwhile, he traveled under the false assumption his persistence would eventually pay off. That delusion ended several days before the couple were scheduled to leave Mexico City for Taxco when Frank – who had learned about the problem from Chris – confronted Kerensky in the men's lavatory at the restaurant where they had met for lunch. Kerensky had gone there to relieve himself and Frank had accompanied him on the same pretext, but with an entirely different motive.

"You little pervert," Frank said and slammed him against the tile wall as soon as the door to the corridor closed. He pinned him there for a moment and then released his grip.

"I'm no pervert," Kerensky replied, shaken but unrepentant. He had the impression something bad was about to happen, which Frank – who was not the least bit angry – wanted him to think.

"If you come within a mile of Christine in my lifetime, I'll beat you into a pulpy mess," he warned Kerensky, who wasn't entirely convinced by the fiction. Frank realized he hadn't gotten his point across, but soon found a more effective measure to convey the message. He took Kerensky by the shoulders and shook him with such violence that his head bobbled up and down until his eyes blurred and his thoughts were rattled. "Do you get my meaning now?" he asked as the teacher backed against the wall and slithered to the floor. "Yes," he replied as Frank left him there to ponder the matter.

Not 15 minutes later, Kerensky rejoined Frank and Chris at their table in the restaurant. He had washed his face, combed his unruly hair and appeared none the worse for his recent experience. "I think I'll have a breast of chicken sandwich and iced tea," he calmly announced.

"The little dunce has balls," Frank thought, but said: "No soup?"

"Not today," was the immediate response, which was followed by a rather awkward silence and then a confession. "I probably shouldn't tell you this, but I think I'd better do it before one of you sends me to the hospital," he began. He went on to tell them he had been retained by a friend of theirs to show them around Mexico City and to let that friend know immediately if there were any signs of trouble. The friend, they quickly determined, was Burt, who had not wanted to dampen their holiday but never-the-less thought some precaution was needed.

"Have you noticed anything unusual?" Frank asked Kerensky. Their former guide seemed to harbor no resentment for the treatment he had experienced at their hands. He seemed to know he deserved it and had put the matter behind him.

"No, but I'm a student of Mexican history and not an intelligence agent," he admitted. He had been recommended to their friend based mainly on his familiarity with the city and its culture. Burt – who with his wife, Fran, was scheduled to meet them later in Acapulco – had tacked on the additional assignment under the assumption a mature, university-educated person had the ability to do the job. He didn't know Kerensky's quirky personality made him a poor choice for the task.

"I think Burt screwed up on this one," Christine said. Kerensky understood what she meant, but showed no offense. Instead, he turned his attention to lunch. "I'm quite hungry," he remarked and elevated a hand to attract a nearby waiter. They subsequently ate lunch together - amiably enough but with sparse conversation-

and then Kerensky left them, timing his departure to avoid the check. They saw him for the last time as they left the restaurant. He had struck up a conversation with a matronly-looking woman – an American tourist, no doubt – and was seated next to her at a table near the entrance. "You look so familiar," they heard him tell her. "I could swear we've met before."

The revelation that Kerensky had been one of Burt's agents surprised Frank, but it also told him their friend was more than likely concerned for Christine's safety. Frank considered Henry Trippa the most likely threat, but he also realized she had cut sharp deals with others in recent years without concern for the possible consequences. For all he knew, there were dozens of malcontented, criminally-inclined people that sought vengeance on Chris who, he thought, placed entirely too much stock in Burt's ability to ensure her safety. It occurred to Frank that Burt could well have lost a step or two with advancing age, and that his selection of Kerensky as a source of intelligence was evidence of his decline. Or, he also thought, he simply picked Kerensky to show them the most interesting things in Mexico City, a task for which he was well qualified and one which had nothing to do with his other deficiencies.

Several days later they were in Cuernavaca, one of the most attractive places in Mexico by virtue of its pink, blue and yellow houses, luxuriant vegetation and colorful flowers. The area, they learned, had been the site of summer residences for everyone from Aztec emperors to the Spanish conqueror, Hernan Cortez, and for later rulers and celebrities of various sorts. Although only a relatively short distance south on the main highway from Mexico City, they had planned to spend the night in Cuernavaca on their way to Taxco where they would linger a few more days before they went on to Acapulco to meet Burt and Fran.

"I have a bad feeling," Christine said as they relaxed on the balcony outside their hotel room and gazed at the red tile roofs so often associated with Cuernavaca. The early evening air was mellow, and bougainvillea with its brilliant purple red blossoms cascaded down the nearby walls.

"You aren't feeling well?" Frank asked. They were both drinking Margaritas, prepared like the cocktails they were meant to be rather than the slushy junk so often sold in North American bars and restaurants.

"No," she corrected. "I have a premonition something bad will happen." She thought for a moment and added: "It's nothing, really."

"You're not nervous about our drive through the mountains, are you?" He asked the question knowing there were few things likely to make her nervous. They had, however, rented a car for the trip from Mexico City to Taxco and then on to Acapulco, which had gone against recommendations, both verbal and printed, about foreigners driving in the country. They had been warned about everything from the Mexican police – who mostly treated gringos as a source of supplemental revenue – to driving at night when various kinds of vehicles, often with only a single headlamp, might swerve into your lane to avoid potholes in theirs. There were also unlighted bicycles and the occasional bandit.

"The mountains don't bother me, and neither do the bandits," she said as a device to change the subject, but the lingering sense persisted that something was either wrong or about to go wrong. That persistence eventually ran its course as they finished their drinks and went off to dinner at a restaurant memorable for its patio setting and the crystalline stars that eventually shown in a dark, cloudless sky. "I can see what the Aztecs saw in this place," Christine observed later on the hotel balcony where they sat for a while before retiring for the night.

The drive to Taxco the next day would have been entirely uneventful had Chris not been afflicted with a gastric disorder reminiscent of their dinner the previous evening. She was genuinely ill when they reached the hotel and barely made it to the room where she dispatched the offensive food and much else into an antique commode. It was not the last effort of that kind for the evening.

"Poor baby," Frank said as he tucked her into bed and went to fetch the medication they had packed for just such an occasion. She had no doubt come down with "Tourista," the bane of North American travelers in Mexico. Given that certainty and administration of the medicine, he assumed she would be better in the morning despite her conviction – rendered in a pitiful voice he had not heard before – that she would surely die in the night. "I doubt it," he reassured her, "but I'll make sure the funeral is a splendid one if I'm wrong."

"Kiss my ass," she replied and fell sound asleep.

"Some other time," he said to himself in deference to her ailment and amused by the thought. He was also surprised to see her so vulnerable and realized, suddenly, that she would not have afforded anyone else that opportunity.

An hour or so later, the phone rang and Frank – who had been reading in a chair near their bed – answered it to find Fran on the other end of the line. "Is Christine there?" she asked. He explained the circumstances and was about to say that Christine would probably be much improved in the morning when Fran interrupted him.

"Burt's had a stroke and he's in a coma," she said, the strain of the circumstance apparent in her voice. "They don't expect him to last the night."

*

Chapter Eight

Alistair Frederick Burton III – who insisted on Burt as a nickname to avoid the alternative, Al – lingered in a coma for several months before he died quietly in the nursing home where his wife, Fran, watched over him with diminishing hope he would regain consciousness and any semblance of his old self. In the end, she was grateful for the death that spared both of them the prospect of his lingering for years in a vegetative state.

In his late 60s when the stroke carried him off, Burt had not expected to die but the event would not have surprised him. He had known for years that life turns on less than a dime, and that the expectation of a long one is, perhaps, a little too optimistic, considering the dangers – everything from terminal disease to heavy traffic – that abound in the world. Given the way he lived his life, he was fortunate to have lived as long as he did.

As Christine vaguely knew, Burt was born into an old, once wealthy Baltimore family that had fallen on hard times before he had an opportunity to profit by their earlier affluence. He and his two sisters had grown up poor but respectable, something his mother had managed after his philandering father disappeared from their lives. The experience taught Burt the maintenance of respectability was only worth the effort when supported by sufficient wealth. Although he was smart to a fault and reasonably well educated for the times in which he lived, the acquisition of money – preferably in large amounts – was his principal goal in life. He could affect interest in other things if it eventually enabled him to show a profit, but he rarely wasted time or effort on anything that didn't connect with one of his many commercial ventures.

Burt was money-driven, but he also had the capacity for close friendships with a select few who showed certain qualities – intelligence, competence and audacity, particularly – that he valued, mainly because he thought those kinds of people were more likely to successfully make their way in the world. Fitz McKenzie, Christine's husband, easily fit that profile, and the two – while not partners in a formal sense – often partnered on deals that extended from the publicly legitimate to the barely legal. They were business sharks who fed at the top of the commercial food chain, and who both accumulated considerable wealth in the process.

"Self interest is my personal interest," Burt told Fitz not long after they met in the early 1920s. "The main difference between me and others like me is that I know it and have no inclination to apologize." And the main difference between the two men was that Fitz – who operated much like his business associate and friend – was not inclined to that much self analysis. He simply sought profit where he could find it under the assumption it was the only rational thing to do. As a consequence, he, too, felt no inclination for apology.

Fitz McKenzie, like Burt, had grown up poor, although he had been genuinely deprived and there was no respectability or earlier wealth attached to his family. His mother and father had immigrated to the United States from the British Isles and settled in west Texas, where they labored at menial jobs that eventually wore them out within months of one another and put them in early graves. An only child orphaned in his teens, Fitz was big and resourceful enough to support himself with odd jobs that soon taught him there were ways to earn a better living.

"I began my business career as a horse thief," he told Burt once they had become friends. "I wasn't very good at it and probably would have wound up in jail or dead if the sheriff in that jurisdiction hadn't been more incompetent than me and the owner of the livestock had been a better shot." He went on to say the experience had been an important lesson in life, one that convinced him to take a different career path. "Not necessarily more honest, just different," he added.

The two men accumulated most of their wealth in various schemes related to real estate and oil, although there were suspicions among the knowledgeable they had financed more secretive projects that varied from gun-running in Central and South America to high priced prostitution in places where there was demand for that sort of thing. They, meanwhile, remained at considerable distance from anything that smacked of illegality and developed over the years a complicated network of international contacts whose reputations ranged from prestigious to murky at best. They were men who not only made money, but knew how to get things done.

"She's a babe," Burt had told Fitz when his friend

asked his opinion about Christine before he proposed marriage. "If you don't marry her, I will." There was the assumption Burt was joking, mainly because he had been married to Fran for some time, and he knew she would more than likely have shot him or worse had he left her for another woman. Burt was originally attracted to Fran for the similarity of their views on many things as well as a nature that matched his for toughness, although disguised by a civilized veneer.

In the end, Burt submerged his physical attraction to Christine, not only because she was married to his best friend and occasional partner and because he was married to Fran, but also because he eventually developed paternal or protective feelings toward the younger woman. As it turned out, Fran, too, learned to like Chris because she was a good companion and – by virtue of her attachment to Fitz – no threat to her own marriage.

"You can call me any time for anything," Burt told Christine after her husband's funeral. By that time, he had learned she was not only an attractive woman but a shrewd operator in her own right, schooled by her husband but with the intelligence and nerve to carry on his various projects. And she soon learned that Burt was a man with immense resources, particularly information about almost anything from high finance to profitable schemes in low places. He could secure impossibly scarce tickets to sold-out sporting events or the services of professionals who were seemingly unavailable to anyone else. He publicly knew congressmen, judges, business tycoons and the merely wealthy as well as others who functioned in enterprises that were nearly illegal or downright criminal. He was a powerful figure who sustained that power without a troop of advisors or thugs, but with a reputation that alerted those who needed to know that he had the resources to do what had to be done. "Thanks, Burt," Christine replied when he made the offer of assistance, barely aware of what he had offered.

"I made the arrangement with Mr. Kerensky," Fran admitted to Christine as they sat in a sunroom at the nursing home where Burt lay deep in a coma on another floor of the building and Frank had gone off to find a coffee machine. "A woman I know had recommended his services."

"I appreciate the thought, but I'd like to unrecommend him," Chris replied, and went on to describe her experience with the horny academic. She had recovered from the gastric disturbance despite their hasty departure from Taxco the morning after they learned about Burt's stroke. They had driven back to Mexico City , caught the first plane to Dallas and made a connection with a flight to Houston.

Christine and Frank remained in Houston with Fran over the months that Burt's comatose body resisted the inevitable drift toward death. On several occasions Chris suggested to Frank that he take a break, perhaps a trip to visit his mother in St. Louis or anything else he cared to do rather than hang around an expensive but essentially depressing nursing facility. "You can surely find something better to do," she said on one occasion.

"If I'm going to be bored, I'd rather be bored in your company," he replied, which was true enough but not the entire story. He was certainly bored with the long hours spent waiting for Burt to give up the ghost, but he knew something Chris didn't know and that information kept him close to her side. Fran had confided in him that Burt – only hours before his stroke – learned that

Henry Trippa had put out a contract on Christine's life. "Burt would have settled the matter, but he ran out of time," Fran told only Frank because she didn't want to worry her friend.

"Let's keep this between us," he suggested and she agreed. Fran, like Burt, had been impressed with Frank's handling of the situation in the Maritime Bar and other revelations about him from Chris had only added to her impression he had extraordinary capacities for a man his age. Mainly, she knew Chris would not likely attach herself to anyone with pedestrian qualities, particularly for as long as she had been with Frank. "What do you propose to do?" Fran asked him.

"I don't yet know," he replied and began to silently review the options available to him. He also retrieved the old .45 from his luggage and began to wear it in a holster on his belt, hidden from view by the sport jacket he also began to wear in public.

Chris, of course, was too observant not to notice the change, especially the pistol, but kept her curiosity in check for some time under the assumption he would explain himself when he saw the need. "You've certainly taken on a sporty aspect," she finally remarked, mostly because the absence of a comment would have ignored the obvious. She realized he was keeping something from her, and it was no great leap to think it had something to do with her security. And given Frank's frequently expressed concern about Henry Trippa, she figured there was probably some connection between his changed behavior and the gangster she had essentially swindled. But she kept these suspicions to herself, although not indefinitely.

"Unless you plan to hunt rabbits with that thing on your belt," she said to him at last, "you could do me the courtesy of revealing that someone, probably Henry Trippa, is out for my scalp." They were at dinner in a small restaurant on an evening Fran had declined an invitation to join them.

"Henry Trippa wants more than your scalp," he admitted between bites of veal scallopini and a seasonal vegetable.

"Is there some reason you couldn't trust me with that information?"

"None," he replied, "except I hadn't decided what to do about it."

"And now?" she inquired.

He put his utensils in the plate and looked directly at her. "Leave Henry Trippa to me," he said. "I'll attend to him shortly." Burt had been buried the day before and they were scheduled to return home before long.

"I'm not afraid of Mr. Trippa," Christine said with complete sincerity.

"I know," Frank acknowledged in a tone that suggested she needed to regard the matter with a little more concern. Privately, he thought she had relied too heavily in the past on Burt's ability to protect her and, even then, seemed to think his powers extended beyond the grave. Actually, she had no such notion. Christine had no fear of Henry Trippa because she simply wasn't afraid of him. She didn't hold him in sufficient regard to cause her any real concern.

Frank was reluctant to discuss his plans for Trippa with Chris because he knew she would attempt to dissuade him, and also because they were incomplete. He needed to return to Florida and learn more about Trippa's daily habits, associates and the layout of his residence, among other things that would govern his eventual course of action. He also wanted to know more about Mr. Hartley who, Frank assumed, was not the only thug on Trippa's payroll. His only assumption at the time was that something forceful had to be done to get the gangster's attention. He had to be shown his lethal plans for Christine weren't worth the pain, physical or financial, it would cause him.

Frank eventually told her that Burt had discovered Trippa's murderous plan, but had not learned anything about the details before his stroke had rendered the whole thing moot for him. Had he not revealed what little he knew to Fran, they would be at an even greater disadvantage than was the case, Frank told Christine.

"I don't need to be sheltered like some flimsy little thing," she said, essentially telling him again she didn't want important information withheld from her. He got the message.

"Next time, you'll be the first to know," he replied. "For now, let's hire a couple of experienced guards – moonlighting cops, perhaps – to watch your house, particularly at night." He made the suggestion as they flew back to Florida aboard a commercial transport. The guards, he explained, could at least provide early warning should anyone try to break into the place. Frank also suggested an expansion of the home alarm system to include the grounds which, he added, might also be rendered safer with the addition of several aggressive dogs. "Rip ass dogs," he said to let her know he wasn't thinking about Lassie.

"I don't want to live like that," was her almost predictable reply, "but I do have an idea." She went on to suggest he buy her a gun – something of appropriate size and weight – and teach her to use it. "That would double our firepower."

Frank bought the idea, but thought it would make a

good addition rather than a substitute for his suggestions. Eventually, however, she would only agree to the expanded alarm system and personal firearms training. “No guards and, particularly, no dogs,” she said. “I’d rather get murdered than have the grounds full of animal poop.”

Frank observed that animal poop was preferable to blood, but knew the matter had been resolved. The following day and with his luggage from the trip still unpacked, he made arrangements to expand the home security system and purchased a small, semi-automatic pistol for Christine. He also set up a compact shooting range in a corner of the property where the sound of gunfire wouldn’t disturb the distant neighbors. His purpose was to thoroughly familiarize her with the weapon, which had limited effectiveness at a distance but provided the prospect of completely different results when properly employed at close range. He taught her not only to fire the gun - using its semi-automatic capacity to put a number of consecutive rounds into a single target – but to maintain it as well. He wanted her to become comfortable with the weapon and to keep it readily at hand.

“This beats the hell out of tennis,” Christine remarked after her first effort with the pistol, which Frank had given her gift wrapped when he returned from the gun store. He was pleased to discover she not only enjoyed shooting, but had a knack for it made possible by keen eyesight and a steady hand. “Zingo,” she said as she peppered the target with holes, two near the bull’s eye.

“Not bad,” Frank observed, aware this phase of his plan would probably be easier than it might have been. He then showed her how to reload the pistol, made some further suggestions on its use and watched as she showed improvement on that day and on succeeding days. Before the week was out, Christine felt quite at home with the weapon she called Zeke. "Fool with me, Mr. Trippa, and Zeke will render your penis to mincemeat," she said aloud to herself as she cleaned the gun after a practice period.

"I'm beginning to think you like that damn thing more than me," Frank said.

"Zeke does turn me on," she replied, "but you have at least one advantage."

"And that is?"

"You're self-cleaning," she explained and stowed the gun in a large handbag she now used for that purpose.

Christine's housekeeper, Angelina, had expressed some misgivings about the pistol and its purpose, but her husband, Jorge, showed more curiosity than concern. He realized there was some reason for a sudden introduction of a firearm into the household, and politely insisted on an explanation. "Angelina and I live here, too," he said, "and we should be told if there is a problem."

"The man has a point," Frank advised Christine in Jorge's presence, and she explained the situation in general terms with the added comment: "There may be a problem, but I don't think anyone's likely to invade the house."

An observant man, Jorge gathered from Frank's activities – everything from the gun range to security system additions – that Christine's dismissal of a possible home invasion might be a tad optimistic. He knew her for the fatalist she was, and had with Angelina often tried to protect her from a host of minor perils she generally ignored. "I have a gun and know how to use it," Jorge told them. "I hope that knowledge will give you some reassurance." He didn't tell them he had been an officer in the army of his native country, forced with his wife into permanent exile as a result of a Marxist revolution that revised their old society and their lives as well.

Frank was inclined to ask Jorge about the kind of weapon he owned and his experience with it, but Christine – who suspected his intent – intervened to express gratitude for the support. She knew Jorge well enough to know he would not have made the offer without the ability to deliver what he had promised. "Thank you," she said.

Frank – who suspected Jorge of competence – meant no disrespect to the man and would only have questioned him out of a natural impulse to gather useful information. Christine's refusal to employ all the defensive means available to them, he felt, stacked the cards in Trippa's favor. As a consequence, he took other measures without consulting her, including an arrangement with the local police department to more closely patrol the area, especially at night. He told the police chief they had received word art thieves had targeted Christine's collection, a blatant lie but more easily explainable than the reality.

Frank had decided to first devise defensive measures against anything Trippa might attempt, and then to go after the man who had created the problem. Without telling Chris, he hired a private detective to watch Trippa's home, mainly to learn about those who lived there or visited with any regularity. He had barely begun to gather the information when a phone call from Nick Satterfield in St. Louis diverted his attention. "Your mother's been in an automobile accident," Nick said. "She's in St. Luke's hospital and I think you need to come home."

Frank thought Nick's use of the word "automobile" rather than "car," which would have been more natural for him, telegraphed the seriousness of the situation. There was something about more formal language that had that effect. "How bad is it?" he asked.

"Pretty bad," Nick replied. He didn't tell Frank his mother was on life support and the attending doctors thought there was little hope she would survive the ordeal. She had been in a head-on collision with a drunk driver whose car was going the wrong way and whose speed at the time of the accident was estimated at more than 90 miles an hour. It had taken the rescue team more than two hours to free her from the mangled wreckage, and the terrible extent of her injuries defied easy description.

"You need to get there as soon as possible, and I'd only be a hindrance," Christine said when he asked her to accompany him on the trip. He was reluctant to leave her behind, but knew there was small likelihood he could convince her otherwise. Instead, he asked her to fly back to Houston, where she could find relative safety with Fran until he could return to Florida. "I'll think about it," was the extent of her commitment.

Several hours later, Frank was at the controls of the Beechcraft, which he flew to Atlanta to make connection with a flight to St. Louis. His former instructor, Bracken, accompanied him that far as co-pilot and then flew the plane back to its home base. The final leg of Frank's flight home was made aboard a DC-3 that lumbered reliably through thickening clouds and finally put down at Lambert Field in a light rainstorm. "She hasn't regained consciousness," were Nick Satterfield's first words when they met in the terminal. He looked as though he hadn't slept or changed clothes for a couple of days, which was the case.

"Does she have a chance?" Frank responded.

"I don't think so, but you never know," Nick said. The grim expression on his face reflected the long odds against his wife's survival.

As Frank endured the hospital vigil for his mother over the next week, the institutional smell of the place and the burdensome monotony of the situation reminded him of the recent death watch for Burt. This time, however, he was also troubled about the danger that confronted Christine and her resistance to the safety measures he thought prudent. "I feel safer at home than in Houston," she told him in the first of daily phone calls he made to her from the hospital in St. Louis. "And I don't think Henry Trippa is smart enough to hurt me."

"God damn it, Christine," he replied with unconstrained annoyance, "he may not be smart, but he's put out a contract on your life. I don't think it takes an intellectual to kill someone."

"I'll be just fine" and "Hurry home, I miss you" or some variation on those two sentiments were all she granted him aside from inquiries about his mother. Frank soon realized the futility of his predicament, and decided to return to Florida if there was no change in his mother's condition within another few days. His long hours at the hospital had given him time to contemplate the problem and he had finally decided his original defensive strategy – given Christine's stubborn refusal to accept all it entailed – was unreliable. He had decided to stop Trippa, dead in his tracks, if necessary.

"Frank, is that you?" a woman's voice aroused him from the thoughts that had consumed his attention. He had been sitting alone in the hospital lounge on a morning Nick had gone home to shower and change clothes.

"It surely is," he replied before he recognized the familiar face, somewhat more mature than the last time he had seen it and altered a bit by a different hair cut. "Molly?' he inquired, aware it wasn't anyone else. He had not seen her since the night they made love for the first time in his old Plymouth.

"I read about the accident in the paper, and guessed that you might be here," she said. "I've often thought about you since we were last together."

"Me, too," he lied spontaneously, although her familiar face restored memories he figured were long forgotten. "You look good," he said and immediately decided he could have expressed himself more gracefully. He also realized he was pleased to see her, although the nature of that pleasure wasn't at all clear to him. "It's been a long time," he added, even more aware his comments were approaching the banal and it really hadn't been that long.

"How's your mother?" she dutifully inquired and sat down next to him on the couch where they commenced a long, restrained conversation that combined reflections on the past and narratives on what they had each done over the few years since they had done it in the back seat of his first car. Molly had delivered on her intention to get married, a union that had lasted little more than a year and was, as she admitted, "a monumental blunder." She described her ex-husband in rather unflattering terms and only referred to his last name, which was Martin, because it was the one she now used. "Molly Martin," Frank said aloud, partially to accustom himself to the sound and partly for the hell of it.

Molly further disclosed she had moved back in with her parents, who had made a move of their own from the old apartment building to a small home in the near suburbs. She now worked as a legal secretary in a downtown law firm, and was half way through an undergraduate program at a local university night school. "I plan to practice law, although I may be a hundred years old before I get the opportunity," she said, not as a complaint but as a simple indication it had been a long, hard slough.

"You'll get there," he assured her. "You've always had a fair notion of what you wanted."

"Perhaps," she replied, "but what I've wanted hasn't always been good for me." The implication she had been wrong about Frank was an apparent come-on, which he treated with an invitation to have dinner with him that evening. He made the invitation on an impulse he barely understood and on the assumption it was harmless enough, at least for the moment.

"Are you attached to anyone?" Frank inquired as they had drinks that evening in a downtown restaurant not far from the office where she was employed. She had taken off work that morning and skipped a later class at the university, something she rarely did.

"I'm so unattached it's a marvel I don't come apart," she replied. "I barely have time to sleep, let alone sleep with anyone."

"Is there any chance you could find time, if it's with the right person?" He had not meant to ask that question, either then or later in the evening when it might have been more appropriate. He was not so much concerned about cheating on Christine as he was about needlessly complicating his own life. He loved Christine and suspected she would allow him an occasional indiscretion – so long as it was sanitary and far from her presence – but he didn't want to risk the possibility of involvement with two women at the same time. Life was complicated enough as it was, he thought.

"I could find time for you," she said directly. "I assume you knew that when I appeared from out of the blue this morning."

"I'm not that smart, at least not where women are concerned," he replied. He had, however, understood what she meant and suggested they have a leisurely dinner and then find a room in a good hotel since she lived with her parents and he was lodged with Nick at his mother's apartment. Frank further explained he would soon return to Florida – where he had urgent business – if there was no change in his mother's condition. He said nothing about the nature of that business, but apologized for rushing her into what he now knew was inevitable.

"You're not rushing me into anything," she explained. "I found you because I still remember what happened in the back seat of your old car. I remember it as if it was yesterday."

"Me, too," he said. This time he spoke the whole truth. Their long discussion had renewed his memory of their relationship, particularly the night in which they coupled for the first and, so far, last time, and she went off to marry some stranger. He recalled the details of her bare body, which had heavily influenced his present decision to do something he suspected was, at the very least, unwise. He particularly remembered her nakedness, softly painted by pale moonlight when they lay together on the cool back seat of his car and she calmly dumped him for someone else.

"You've learned a few things since we last did this," Molly remarked later as she nestled against his chest. The spread and top sheet had been pushed to the foot of the large hotel bed, where it lay crumpled on the carpet.

"I'd be a sorry specimen if I hadn't," was the response. "I didn't know anything then." He didn't tell her all his sexual experience derived from Christine. In fact, he didn't tell her anything about Christine. No need to further complicate an already complicated situation, he reasoned later when he thought about it. Meanwhile, he told her he was bound to return to St. Louis, given his mother's condition, but the timing of the trip would depend on her situation as well as the disposition of his business in south Florida. He had decided to leave the next day, and was about to disclose his intention when she began to gently kiss his chest. "I don't expect anything from you," she said quietly, although he had not thought she did. The progression of her kisses distracted his thoughts of travel and would eventually convince him they should see each other again. He understood his attraction to the woman was to a great extent sexual, but he also sensed a bond between them that went back to their teenage connection. There was, he came to suspect, some essential chemistry that remained, but he put the matter aside in order to clear his thoughts for more immediate concerns.

"It's been more than good to see you," he said to Molly when he left her on her parent's doorstep late that night. "I'd like to see you again."

"Me, too," she said this time. She suspected there were complicating factors in his life he had not disclosed, and assumed at least one had something to do with a woman. That conclusion was entirely reasonable, given his age, vitality and the inclination he had demonstrated that very evening. “It’s been more than I probably deserve,” she added, but without the slightest sense of guilt. Her allusion – which he understood – was to the fact she had once dumped him, but she – much like Frank – was not inclined to wallow in regret. They kissed goodnight and each wondered if or when they would meet again.

*

Chapter Nine

"I doubt if art theft had anything to do with this," the detective told Frank, who had not yet come to accept the reality of what had happened. Christine was dead and so were Angelina and Jorge, all murdered with individual shotgun blasts at close range. And the art work – which Frank had used as a pretext to get regular police patrols of the area – was untouched. He would soon learn that two of the criminal assailants were also dead, one shot by Christine and the other by Jorge. And one of the corpses was Mr. Hartley, who had taken two slugs to his face from Christine's small pistol.

"The art collection was not important enough to justify anything more than a small burglary," Frank told the officer, "and there was nothing else in the house of great value." He knew, of course, who had sponsored the attack, but kept that knowledge to himself, unwilling to leave justice to a system he thought was riddled with cumbersome uncertainty. He had also arrived in Florida from St. Louis only hours after the assault and was, himself, a suspect until somewhat later when the police were able to determine his presence aboard a southbound airliner when the murderous events took place. At the time, he was not only thousands of feet above the ground but surrounded by witnesses in the first class section of the plane. One of the stewardesses had, in fact, paid him particular attention against the possibility he was unmarried and unattached in any other way.

The police eventually determined there had been four attackers, including the dead ones and two survivors who had clumsily blasted their way into the place with shotguns and with no expectation there would be any defense against them, particularly from two women and a middle-aged male house servant. They had succeeded in killing their target, Christine, but the miscalculation had cost them dearly and the pronounced skid marks outside the front gate showed they had left in a great hurry. The police investigation would eventually identify the two survivors through their association with the late Mr. Hartley, but by that time they, too, were dead under circumstances that compounded the general mystery.

The invaders had intended to kill everyone on the premises and leave no witnesses to the crime, an intention that was apparent in the shooting of Angelina, who was the first to die only because she was the first one they met inside the house. The single shotgun blast that ended her life, however, alerted Christine and Jorge to the assault and gave them time to retrieve their weapons.

Frank was denied access to the house – where the three distinct murder scenes were a chaotic combination of blood-stippled, pellet-riddled walls and various kinds of shards – but was later asked to identify the bodies. Both Angelina and Jorge had taken direct frontal blasts and were barely recognizable, but Christine had received a lower shot, more than sufficient to kill her instantly but one that left her pretty face intact. “Goodbye, sweetheart,” Frank said to himself as the coroner’s assistant replaced the cover over her lifeless body. Frank’s other thoughts were mostly expletive-laden ones directed at Henry Trippa, but he fought to retain his composure in the presence of the police and their confederates. He was able to stifle the enormous surge of hatred that threatened to overwhelm him only because he knew there was no other way he would achieve revenge. “Stay cool,” he told himself more than once.

In a phone call to Fran in Houston – who had almost expected the news based on her knowledge of the contract put out on Christine’s life – Frank explained the circumstances that had kept him away when the attack occurred. “Don’t blame yourself,” Fran advised.

“I don’t,” Frank replied. “I know who to blame.” The tone of his voice told her he was not likely to let the criminal justice system dispose of the case. She offered assistance, particularly in the form of several men Burt had called on from time to time to resolve sticky matters that were somewhat beyond legal solution. “They’re tough, discreet and owe Burt more than they can ever repay,” she said, implying she was willing to call in the debts.

“I appreciate the offer but the wheels of retribution are already in motion,” he told her before she wished him luck and they ended the conversation. “The wheels” in his allusion was the plan that would unfold over the next week as Frank assembled information from the private detective he had hired earlier and equipment he had acquired to achieve a single objective, a personal confrontation with Henry Trippa.

Unable as a result of the police investigation to stay in

Christine's house and unwilling to ever see the place again, Frank moved into a single room at a modest motel and clandestinely purchased with cash an unobtrusive garage-like structure in a distant run-down industrial park. Before the murders were a week old, he knew in significant detail the lay-out of Trippa's house and had information about its occupants and visitors from the private investigator's report he had commissioned before the crimes were committed. He had assembled several weapons and paraphernalia at the garage, where he also parked a plain but dependable old car he had acquired in another cash transaction. His residence at the motel was no secret, but his efforts at the garage and elsewhere in connection with the plan were carried out with great care, often at night, to avoid police scrutiny. In any case, he had been removed from the list of prime suspects once the details of his trip to St. Louis and his presence aboard the airliner had been confirmed. These facts alone probably wouldn't have been sufficient to remove police suspicion had they known he was sole heir to Christine's substantial fortune, although even Frank had failed to understand that fact at the time. She had told him in plain enough language he was her inheritor, but he had not taken the revelation seriously. Later when the police discovered this information, the investigation had made clear he could not have either committed or sponsored the crimes.

"You're wealthy beyond your wildest dreams," Fran told Frank during a subsequent phone call in which she revealed the substance of Christine's will. She was the executor and had originally opposed the decision that now made Frank a multi-millionaire. She told him as much, but went on to explain she had changed her mind in that regard.

"My dreams aren't particularly wild, but my conscious thoughts are something else entirely," he replied. He also told her he, too, would have been against his inclusion in the will, but supposed he was there by default. "There wasn't anyone else," he added.

Christine's will stipulated cremation for her remains and dispersal of the ashes over the Gulf of Mexico, Fran told him. "I think that body of water came as close to home for her as any place else," she said.

"It beats North Tonawanda, New York," Frank responded, recalling the industrial town where Chris grew up and fled as a very young woman. He agreed the Gulf was the most appropriate place to strewn her ashes, preferably as the sun set, and said he would handle the responsibility himself rather than consigning it to one of the commercial services in the area. "Care to join me?" he asked.

Fran agreed to accompany Frank on the flight, which he told her would take place after he had settled certain matters she now understood were in the immediate offing. "I don't expect it will take very long," he had said, almost as if it were preordained. Frank wasn't the sort to underestimate a difficult task, but he had been surprised by the rather casual atmosphere his reports on Henry Trippa's residence and schedule had revealed. The man lived alone, although guarded by a couple of thugs that were probably, Frank suspected, the two survivors of the attack on Christine's home. There were occasional women – more than likely prostitutes – who spent time with Trippa, but predictably on weekends when he often took his boat out for shot cruises to nowhere in particular. Most nights, he ate dinner in a nearby restaurant with the two men who guarded his house, but Trippa was always home no later than 10 o'clock.

"He doesn't know that Burt got wind of the contract on Christine's life, and thinks he's in the clear," Frank concluded. He also figured Trippa thought his two guards were sufficient for what little threat there was to a man who always carried his own gun and knew how to use it. But that same man – tough enough not only to survive but to rise in the criminal world when he was younger – had grown soft with time and relative prosperity, although he had failed to recognize the change. "I doubt he even remembers me," Frank thought, and wondered why Trippa had finally decided to use his own incompetent thugs for the murders rather than let the lethal contract induce some outsider to do the job.

The police investigators later determined that Henry Trippa's death along with his two associates was probably the result of some internecine struggle among local criminal gangs, and eventually closed the file without a more definitive conclusion. The authorities – at least those who had dealt with him – seemed genuinely pleased to have him gone, mostly because his obnoxious personality over the years had been even more objectionable than the various crimes he had committed with more impunity than was consistent with any degree of justice. And while the police were eventually able to develop suspicions that Trippa's two associates may have been involved in the assault on Christine's home, the evidence was fragile and they were never able to connect the dead gangster with the crime. As a result, that case, too, went into limbo, although there was no statute of limitations on capital crimes.

The death of Henry Trippa produced no mourners, but

the detectives who investigated the case and others on the police force who learned about it were taken with the brutal precision with which the executions were carried out. Trippa's two associates had been dispatched quickly in separate parts of the large house – each with broken necks that had sent them instantly to some great beyond – but their boss had suffered a lingering and painful death. He had been beaten like an old rug and then, bound tightly, hung by his feet from one of the exposed rafters in his mock English Tudor living room. As he slowly but consciously died from the wounds inflicted on him, his killer carved painful slashes on particularly sensitive parts of his body until at last he bled out onto the gaudy, rust-colored caret below him. The police report noted his mouth had been taped shut, denying him the screams of agony that might have provided some minimal relief from the experience. "I suspect," one of the investigators remarked when he saw the body, "that he made somebody mad."

Unlike the usual gangland killings – where the target was simply assassinated in a hail of gunfire on a public street or in some public venue like a restaurant or barber shop – this one, despite its primitive brutality, had been carefully planned and carried out with extraordinary deliberation. There was no sign of forced entry and not a single piece of physical evidence, not a blurred fingerprint or a stray hair. And there was not a trace of blood other than the great pool that had accumulated under Trippa's body. The lead detective on the case suspected several people had been brought in from out of town to do the job. "The local guys just aren't that good," he reasoned.

Several days after Trippa's ripe remains were discovered by the woman who cleaned his house, Frank

Bonner piloted a rented Cessna 172 off the runway and into a cloudless sky that would soon darken as the sun set over the Gulf of Mexico. Grady Bracken sat next to him in the four-place aircraft and Fran occupied one of the two back seats, holding urns that contained the ashes of Christine, Angelina and Jorge. Since the couple's burial preference was unknown, Frank had elected to commit their remains to the Gulf along with those of Christine. "It's a perfect evening," Fran observed as the plane gained altitude and took a westward heading toward the Gulf.

"I feel like a witness to the extinction of human life on earth," Frank told Fran several days later when he learned in a phone call from Nick Satterfield that his mother had died without emerging from her coma. The deaths of Burt, Christine and his mother in such rapid succession seemed like "some ridiculous accident, something that could be reversed or repealed if there was any justice in the world or any reasonable God," he added.

"I gave up years ago on any expectation of a reasonable world," Fran said and advised him to go home and bury his mother. She and Frank had begun work on the legalities and other things attached to Christine's complicated estate, which she would continue while he attended to matters in St. Louis. An adaptable person, Fran had settled comfortably into a suite at the best hotel in the area, where she set up a temporary office from which to conduct the business that would eventually transfer the McKenzie wealth to Frank. At that point, he had only the vaguest inkling of his new circumstances.

With Bracken as his co-pilot, Frank flew the Beechcraft to St. Louis mainly to avoid the vacant hours that a commercial flight would have imposed on him. He preferred to busy himself at the controls of a plane that would soon be legally his rather than sit idly as a passenger on an airliner piloted by someone else. He had easily induced Bracken to join him with only the prospect of a change of scene, although he suggested they might try to seek out Bill Hager, the crusty old pilot and owner of Hager's Field they both knew from earlier times. Bracken understood, however, that he would have to fend for himself until Frank was able to navigate the ceremonial course imposed by the death of a close relative. In this case, Nick Satterfield had made arrangements for a church service and burial in a formal cemetery, one that had no connection to Frank's family or to anyone or anything else he could determine.

"I suspect my mother believed in God or something similar, but she never to my knowledge went to church," Frank told Nick, mostly in an effort to understand why he had decided on a church service and formal burial for a woman who had not shown a great deal of interest in religion during her lifetime.

"She usually worked on Sundays, but she went to church on Christmas and Easter, and you could bank on it," Nick informed him.

"You're kidding," Frank said, aware he wasn't, and wondering how something so basic had escaped his notice. He could not imagine his mother in church, and wondered why she had not imposed religion on him when he was a boy. "Better not to look a gift horse in the mouth . . . or anywhere else, for that matter," he thought.

Frank offered to assist Nick with the arrangements, but discovered most of the work had been done by the time he arrived in St. Louis. He also insisted on covering the expense of the funeral, but Nick would only allow him to split the costs. “It’s not a matter of money,” Nick explained.

“I know,” Frank replied, “but there’s no reason for you to take on the obligation when I’ve got more of the stuff than I’ll ever need.” He told Nick about his acquisition of Christine’s estate, but had the impression his step-father failed to grasp the full extent of his new wealth. In any case, he finally realized his ability to pay for things had nothing to do with Nick’s insistence on sharing the expense. The division of responsibility was based on their shared love for the dead woman, and the financial consideration was only an unimportant symbol of something more significant. “That was probably a little lesson in life,” Frank thought later when he had time to consider the matter. He had learned from Christine and Burt that money, properly deployed, bestowed everything from power to leisure on those who had it, but Nick had reminded him there were areas where it had little, if any, application. The trick, he began to realize, was to know the difference.

“I can smell that sweet stuff,” Ann Richardson, known as Rock House Annie after a club near grungy East St. Louis, Illinois where she had performed for years, said to Frank, who with Nick and Bracken had stopped at the Barrel Bar for a drink several hours after the funeral. Ann had mistaken the aroma of plain cigarette smoke, which hung in the air like an impenetrable fog, for something less legal and more intoxicating.

“I don’t smell a thing,” Frank replied, an implication his nasal passages had been shut down by the abundance of smells, including beer, liquor, tobacco, human perspiration and some that were fortunately indefinable in the long, narrow barroom where Ann sang and manipulated a responsive audience of mostly young people several nights a week. A tall, black woman who wore long, skin-tight dresses that favored her remarkable 50-year-old figure, Ann Richardson's smoky voice was locally famous, as was her regular on- stage admonition. "If I can't sell it, I'll sit on it. I ain't gonna give it away," she would say, and then turn her back on the audience in order to arch a prodigious behind in their direction. Her crisp pronouncement of the words "ain't" and "gonna" told anyone with a keen ear for language that her use of those corrupted words were mere devices for their entertainment and had nothing to do with her natural mode of speech.

"Well, it doesn't hurt to ask," she advised anyone within earshot and made her way conversationally down the bar until it was time for the next set.

"I'd marry that woman in a minute," Bracken observed as he watched her work the customers in a routine that had become as much a part of her persona as the ample cleavage revealed by the neckline of her gown. The off-stage chatter with her audience was simply an extension of the on-stage performance, something she did to maintain control of a fickle crowd whose attention could easily be diverted by almost anything.

"I'll be your best man," Nick offered as the three of them found a small table just short of a hall that led to the lavatories. Bracken had accompanied Frank to the funeral, where he met Nick, who later suggested they have dinner together. And still later, he suggested to Frank they show Bracken the bars along several blocks of Delmar Boulevard between Goodfellow to the west and Clara Avenue to the east where several varieties of jazz were played, especially on Friday and Saturday nights before blue laws extinguished the music early on Sunday mornings. These places bore names like The Mainline and The Windermere as well as The Barrel and with several others formed a smaller less notable version of the entertainment district along New York's 52nd Street.

Aside from a toast to Frank's late mother and Nick's wife – which was accomplished by clinking their beer bottles together – the three men talked about nothing in particular as new customers crowded the skinny barroom and the noise level between musical sets reached a point that threatened permanent hearing loss. Despite the ordinary nature of their conversation and some difficulty in hearing one another, Nick gleaned some idea, particularly from several of Bracken's offhand remarks, that Frank had not exaggerated his material circumstances.

"Just how flush is my step-son?" Nick asked Bracken when Frank had gone to the men's room, more to escape the rising level of smoke than to relieve himself.

"I don't know," Bracken replied truthfully but also with reluctance to reveal that kind of information without Frank's knowledge, "but he's probably the richest man I know." Bracken didn't tell him he knew some very rich men, who he had met over the years in the course of piloting their private aircraft. He only disclosed that opinion because Frank had spoken well of Nick, which told Bracken he could be trusted. Later and when they were alone, Nick's curiosity about the source of Frank's wealth would prompt him to question his step-son, who told him about Christine and the circumstances of her death. "Have they," meaning the police, "found the killers?" Nick asked.

"The killers are dead," Frank replied and changed the

subject. Nick, who had sponsored Frank's early martial arts training, knew something of his capacities and understood in general terms that the matter had been settled out of court. "I'm sorry about Christine," he said and then went along willingly with the change of subject.

Frank left Bracken in Nick's care the following evening when he met Molly for dinner, an engagement he made with her by phone earlier that day. "I don't have classes this evening," she informed him, although they both knew she would have skipped school had it been otherwise. He had reached her at the office where she worked and did not disclose an earlier call to her parent's home the previous evening. He had used the public phone outside the men's room at the Barrel Bar, but she had not yet returnd from her university class. To Frank's surprise, the call had been answered by a child, a boy who candidly told him his mother was away before Molly's own mother retrieved the instrument and told him the very same thing.

"What's your name?" Frank asked the boy before his grandmother intervened.

"Frankie," was the response. "Frankie Martin."

Despite the brevity of their conversation, Frank had discovered that Molly was the mother of a son, probably, he judged by the boy's voice, about seven or eight years old. The revelation had stirred his thoughts well into the next day when he called Molly, but he kept the matter to himself until they were together for dinner.

"You've got a son?" he inquired after they had been seated at the restaurant and before the waiter appeared to take a drink order.

"Yes," she replied, not surprised by the question because her mother had told her about the events related to his call. Her mother didn't know Frank wasn't aware Molly had a son. And she also had no idea Frank and Molly had been intimate within a time frame that made him wonder about the boy's paternity. "I wistfully named him Frank because I missed you and detested the man I married," she confessed.

"Am I the father?"

"I don't know," Molly admitted, although she said it was entirely possible. Her marriage and physical relationship with her ex-husband had been short-lived, but it had happened not long after she and Frank had done it in the back seat of the old Plymouth. "I hope he's yours because I don't like the alternative." Molly went on to say she wouldn't try to impose any obligation on him. "It wouldn't be fair," she added.

"Who said life was fair," he said as the waiter arrived and took their drink orders. Frank had pondered the possibility he might be a father based on his estimate of the boy's age and, perhaps, an unconscious effort to establish a connection with a woman he had always loved despite his attachment to Christine. Strangely, he had either understood or tolerated Molly's defection to another man, and had never held it against her. He had always figured she would have married him had he been willing at the time. Although he had not sorted out his intentions toward Molly, he knew he wanted her and the son – whether the boy was his or not – to have secure and comfortable lives. "I have a plan," he told her and laid out a proposal in which he would provide the means for her to quit work and finish school. He meant to buy a small house for her and supply an income sufficient for reasonable needs. He was careful to make the offer appear modest, assuming, correctly, she would be put off by the implication of excess.

"You're kidding?" was her response, mostly because

she thought the offer was beyond his means.

"Nope," he assured her. He explained convincingly that his resources had compounded considerably since her son had been "mysteriously conceived," but he didn't attempt to describe the full extent of that improvement. He only wanted her to know he could easily supply the support, and that it would not impose the least bit of financial hardship on him. "You can have the money in a lump sum or in monthly installments, but there's only one thing I want in return," he said.

"And that is?"

"I want to meet the boy, son or not," her replied. "I'm anxious to see him and I don't care if the father is the King of Siam."

"The father, more than likely, was the owner of an old Plymouth," she said in an allusion to his first car but inadvertently revealing she thought Frank was, indeed, the male parent. She hadn't revealed that conviction before because she couldn't prove it and didn't want to force an obligation on him. But she also saw in the boy a physical resemblance to Frank, although that impression, she understood, could well have been the product of wishful thinking.

By the end of dinner – which had been preceded by a couple of leisurely drinks – he had convinced her to at least give the proposal some thought. "You'll be a better mother and student if you take the offer," he suggested in an effort to clinch the sale.

"I'd also owe you more than I could pay back in a generation," she pointed out.

"Not necessarily, he countered. "I could extract the obligation from your good looking body." He thought for a moment his remark – meant, of course, as something resembling a joke – had struck the wrong note until she replied: "Why would you pay for something you could get for nothing?"

Later in the same hotel as well as the same room where they had done it before, he asked as they lay next to one another if she had considered an abortion when she discovered her pregnancy. "You hated your husband and I was nowhere in sight," Frank said to justify his question. He wondered if she had been restrained by religious or some other anti-abortion sentiment.

"I don't like abortions, but I hope it's legal some day," she explained. "Banning the procedure doesn't stop it. It only makes it dangerous." She didn't tell him she had a young friend who had died following an illegal, back-alley abortion performed by some medical hack. "Anyway, I wanted the child and I've never been sorry," Molly said.

They spent the night together and had breakfast in the dining room the next morning before she went off to work, aware he would fly back to Florida that day but return within a week or two to meet her son. She had brought a change of clothes with her – neatly concealed in a large handbag – when they met for dinner the prior evening, which told Frank she had the capacity to anticipate events. He liked the event she had anticipated as well as her company afterward, which also told him the attraction, at least as far as he was concerned, was more than physical. "How much more and where it would lead?" was the question that he put off until later because it was something that didn't need instant resolution.

With Frank at the controls and Bracken in the co-pilot's seat, the Beechcraft was airborne shortly after noon on a course that took it across the Mississippi

River to nearby Hager Field where they hoped to find its owner. Bracken had tried unsuccessfully to identify a phone number for the airport and they finally decided to fly a few miles out of their way to see if Bill Hager still ran the field. "The old bastard is probably dead and buried in a pile of airplane wreckage," Bracken observed.

Frank had not been to Hager Field since the day he sold the Stearman, but he had no need to consult charts to find the airport, situated as it was just beyond the great river and a large curved lake on the Illinois side where migratory waterfowl gathered on their seasonal flights up and down the ancient waterway. "That should be it over there," he said to Bracken, who peered into the near distance at an altitude that would soon put them into the landing pattern.

"I see a runway, but damn little else," Bracken noted, and Frank soon realized that a single landing strip was all that remained of the old field. There was no sign of the hangar where he had worked as a boy or the odd assortment of other small buildings that had composed the airport. "Damn," Frank said wistfully, taking the Beechcraft down to within several hundred feet of the ground and circling the area for a closer view of what was nothing more than a large grassy field with a crumbling runway that had always been too short for anything but relatively small planes. "I guess we can kiss Bill Hager goodbye." He then piloted the plane into a heading toward their Florida destination and sought sufficient altitude for the long trip.

*

Chapter Ten

"I can barely believe she's been dead five years," Fran said to Frank on the anniversary of Christine's death. They had met for dinner at a Houston country club for the purpose of remembering her friend and his benefactor. "In fact, I can't believe she's dead and I'm still alive," she added. Her hair had gone from gray to almost white in the period since Christine's death, but she was otherwise unchanged. Her aging body remained lean and her mind – which Frank had learned to appreciate for its business acumen and clarity of thought – had not lost a step.

"I suspect you'll live forever," Frank observed.

"There's the possibility I already have." Her remark was made with a mixture of humor and the vague awareness most of her life was over.

Although Fran lived in the Houston area and rarely traveled any more while Frank rarely stayed in one place for very long, they had established a strong friendship and business arrangement that kept them in regular touch with one another. Fran had mentored Frank in a variety of enterprises, using not only her experience and good sense, but the global contacts that had been developed over many years by her late husband, Burt.

They reminisced at length about Christine over cocktails and dinner as they had often done since her death, but inevitably their conversation turned to other matters. "Anything new with Peregrine?" Fran inquired about the small airline Frank had begun several years earlier and which now had a fleet of several dozen planes that hauled almost anything transportable by air to almost anywhere in the western hemisphere. He had named the company Peregrine Airways after the falcon, which is not only the fastest animal in the world – capable of speeds that exceed 200 miles an hour in a dive – but one that can be found almost everywhere on earth, excluding those regions that are either too hot or too cold.

"It's in the black, thanks to you," he replied. He meant that her contacts had enabled him to secure business from several national governments and a number of corporations to fly various cargoes, some quite ordinary but others of a clandestine nature.

"Don't be modest," she replied. "You've done a remarkable job in no time at all."

He had, indeed, put together a small but efficient airline in an informal partnership with Grady Bracken, whose wide experience with transport aircraft and his friendships with veteran pilots had been essential to the acquisition of equipment and experienced personnel. Although the company had smaller planes in its fleet, most were Douglas DC-3s. This twin-engine, propeller-driven piece of aviation history had revolutionized air transportation in the 1930s and 40s, and its military version or C-47 had been more than useful to the Allied cause in the Second World War. The Peregrine logo – a vigilant hawk – was stenciled inconspicuously on most of the planes, although some were left unmarked by anything other than the mandatory registration numbers.

"I understand you've actually done some of the flying," she continued. "Don't you have better things to do, and professional pilots to handle that sort of thing?" She was concerned about his safety and also thought he might be paying too little attention to his substantial real estate and other investments.

"I'm not an office animal," he explained. He also told her that he usually took control of planes taking him to business destinations, which was an evasion of the full truth. He often piloted the business flights, of course, but he also liked to fly occasional runs with secret cargos to dangerous or interesting places. He had flown guns into unpublicized war zones, and transported celebrities seeking privacy and space they could not achieve on either regular commercial flights or on smaller chartered aircraft. Meanwhile, Frank had begun to accumulate a great deal of flying time, and was considered a peer by the skilled pilots who worked for him.

Bracken, too, had come to respect Frank, not only for his competence as a pilot but for his general qualities as well. But the older man's natural prudence – which had enabled him to survive in an occupation rife with hazards – thought his partner took too many chances, particularly ones he could have delegated to others. Frank had once flown a lumbering DC-3 onto a short jungle airstrip to deliver weapons and explosive materials to beleaguered guerilla fighters seeking the overthrow of a despotic government, and barely made it out of the place, his plane riddled with bullet holes. And not long afterward he landed a smaller aircraft on the slope of a mountain to provision a team of rescuers who had been cut off from assistance by an avalanche and was stranded with them for days until help arrived from the outside world. Bracken attributed this behavior to simple recklessness, an inbred need for adventure or, at least, something to hone the dull edge off everyday life. There was no doubt some truth in that assumption, but he didn't realize – and Frank was unlikely to tell him – that the main reason was quite different.

"I hate bullies," Frank once told Bracken, who had narrowly interpreted the remark to mean nasty individuals who picked on others – inevitably weaker than themselves – for no good reasons. There was some truth in that, too, but Frank in his maturity had come to think in much broader terms. The bullies he hated most were small-time dictators, rapacious business tycoons and certain industries that operated with little concern for the vulnerable public. "I like to take an occasional shot at those bastards," he had also told Bracken, who failed to understand that Frank's flight onto the jungle airstrip had more to do with his attitude toward a brutally corrupt government than it did with the need for personal adventure. And other episodes – like the landing on a mountain slope – were done because Frank saw merit in rescuing a group of rescuers. He also saw irony in the eventual need for his own rescue.

Fran lectured him at some length through their meal about his wayward habits, aware he was unlikely to change and that her instructions in that regard were entirely futile. "You haven't heard a word I've said," she said at last.

"Not true," he replied. "I always listen to you." He meant he listened to her advice about practical matters and generally ignored her suggestions about more personal ones. He had told Fran a couple of years earlier about his relationship with Molly – who had since graduated law school and was working as an assistant prosecuting attorney – and she had subsequently advised him to marry the woman. Frank didn't know that Fran had run an investigation on Molly, whose virtues – industriousness and others – were more profound than he would have guessed. Frank was still attracted by her straight-forward nature, good looks and sexual proclivities. He had also established a relationship with the son who might or might not be his, and managed to spend time with the boy – who was now an early teenager – and his mother whenever business or inclination sent him in their direction.

"You need to wed that woman," Fran advised him again before the evening was over. The advice was based on her conviction that marriage would settle him down, at least to some extent, and probably get him to focus on things other than the airline. Actually, Frank paid close attention to all his enterprises and Fran simply failed to acknowledge that she feared his excessive flying would one day put him at the controls of a crashed airplane in some vast wilderness.

"I've thought about it," he told Fran in connection with her suggestion he marry Molly.

"Well?" she asked.

"I'm still thinking about it," he said in an attempt to make the truth sound more jocular.

Actually, he had thought about Molly and her son, Frankie, in a familial way for some time, but had not been able to conclude that marriage would serve any useful purpose for anyone. The boy knew him as "Uncle Frank," something akin to a distant father who showed up from time to time with great gifts and took him to any reasonable place he wanted to go, providing he got his mother's permission . Frankie probably would have liked Frank in any event, but the man's access to airplanes and other privileges went a long way toward securing the boy's affection. On the other hand, Frank liked Frankie, too, as he got to know him and discovered the boy had certain qualities he admired, including smartness and grit. Molly had recognized those traits in her son and concluded they derived from Frank, who was inclined to give her the credit for the young man's virtues.

Molly's ex-husband, Joe Martin, had never shown interest in the boy, mainly because she had told him Frank was the biological father. She, of course, was uncertain about Frankie's paternity, but wanted to distance her son from a man who had abused her both physically and emotionally in the short period of their marriage. He had also returned to her life from time to time, usually in the form of menacing phone calls, until she got a legal restraining order that modified his behavior to some extent.

"What's wrong?" Frank asked Molly on an evening when he was in town and they had elected to spend time together in the house he had acquired for her some years earlier.

"Nothing important," she replied.

"What's wrong that's not important?" he persisted, and she told him Joe Martin had called her several times in the past month seeking money he claimed she had withheld during their marriage. Martin assumed, Molly told Frank, that her ability to buy a house and finance an education was evidence she had cheated him out of something that was rightfully his. "The only trouble with his theory is that we didn't have a damn thing when we were married, not a spare penny," she said. "He was a lousy provider and a mean person."

"How mean?"

"Mean enough," she replied, unwilling to provide the humiliating details, which Frank was able to surmise in general terms. He had not known that Martin had been physically abusive to Molly. "Anyway," she continued, "I'm an assistant prosecutor now, and he'll go to jail if he violates the restraining order." She had made an effort to sound confident, but Frank discerned from her troubled manner a certain lack of confidence in the legal system she represented. He knew from experience that some people – men like Joe Martin, possibly – were not easily restrained by legal orders. They could only be controlled, he felt, by force, legal or otherwise.

"Is he living in the area?" Frank asked, wondering how close the physical threat was to Molly and her son.

"He's not a problem," Molly said, diverting the question in an effort to remove Frank's concern, which was apparent. She didn't want her problem to become his problem, unaware it was too late and that Frank had resolved to settle the matter.

Joe Martin was not entirely a thug and could, when it suited his purpose, display a certain amount of amiability toward men or charm where women were concerned. It was the latter quality that had enabled him to successfully court Molly, but it was only a superficial trait that did not last beyond the first few months of their marriage when his abusive nature came to the surface. She left him soon after that, aware she was pregnant but smart enough to know the two problems – her husband and her condition – were completely incompatible.

Martin – Frank learned from one of his investigative sources – had sustained himself modestly with a succession of minor sales jobs, occasionally out of St.

Louis, but mostly in the metropolitan area. At the time, he had a small apartment in a declining suburb and drove an older sedan that showed signs of neglect. Frank also discovered that Martin had the habit of casing Molly's house, usually by parking his car down the street and observing her movements from some distance with binoculars. This behavior alone, Frank concluded, was evidence of impending trouble, something that called for a remedy beyond persuasive conversation.

A large man by most standards, Martin assumed his size gave him a certain amount of authority over men of lesser stature and any woman who came into his life in a more than casual way. But he was not a fighter, either by nature or training, a fact that eluded him because circumstance had never taught him that reality. He simply assumed he was the physical superior of anyone smaller. That was his general conviction when Frank Bonner confronted him on the deserted parking lot of a neighborhood tavern a few blocks from his apartment. The wind was rising on an early fall evening, and the scent of rain was in the air. Martin had just finished his customary two beers after work and was on his way home.

"I want a word with you," Frank said.

"Do I know you?" Martin's manner was reasonable enough because he had not yet learned the nature of the "word" he was about to hear.

"I'm a friend of Molly's and I'm not here for a discussion," Frank explained. "I'm going to beat the crap out of you, and if you ever bother her again I'll kill you."

"You're going to what?" was all Martin was able to say before Frank's right fist slammed into his stomach. As he doubled over in pain and surprise, a second blow broke his nose and was followed by a kick to the groin that inflicted more anguish than damage as he crumpled to the asphalt pavement.

“Do you understand?” Frank inquired as Martin stared blankly at him, groaning in something that approached agony. He didn’t respond and Frank inflicted two broken ribs on the man with a single, targeted kick. “Do you understand?” he repeated. Martin was still unable to muster a verbal answer, but he shook his head in assent as his eyes registered disbelief at what had just happened to him.

“One other thing,” Frank said before he left Martin, now curled into a near fetal position on the ground. “If you report this matter to anyone other than your bookie, you’ll see me or one of my friends again.” Martin made it home with great difficulty that evening and moved to a more secretive place as soon as he was sufficiently healed.

“The restraining order apparently worked,” Molly advised Frank a number of weeks later when he returned to St. Louis. “I haven’t heard a peep out of Joe.”

“You’ve restored my faith in the legal system,” he replied. He also preferred to maintain her faith in that system and to hide the violence that had been employed to keep her safe. He was reasonably certain she wouldn’t have approved had the full truth about Joe Martin’s treatment been available to her. She hated violence, he knew, just as he hated people, mostly men, who use violence against those who don’t deserve that attention. He hated it so much it sometimes drove him to violence.

Frank still had something of a philosophical dilemma

where violence was concerned. He thought the use of force toward good ends was not only effective and morally justifiable, but the only solution to some problems. At the same time, he didn't like that necessity and wished reason and decent behavior were the means more often employed to handle matters that were mostly resolved by conflict. "I'll have to live with the ambiguities," he thought, but without regret for the beating he had imposed on Joe Martin.

In Florida a few months later, Frank had forgotten Joe Martin and was occupied with his usual business matters when he received a phone call on a private line with a number known only to a select few, among them Fran and Nick Satterfield. And while the caller's voice seemed distantly familiar, Frank realized at once it was someone other than those who had been given the number. "Who is this?" was his predictable question.

"It's Jack, you bloody fool," the caller said.

"Jack who?" Frank asked, just as he figured out the voice was either Jack Smiley or more than a reasonable facsimile. "Is that really you, Jack?"

"Nobody else," the caller confirmed, "although I wouldn't have been that confident about my identity a year ago." It was, indeed, Jack Smiley, who explained an exploding artillery shell at the Battle of Chosin Reservoir in Korea had severely wounded him and caused a concussion that wiped out his memory. "I didn't know myself from Mao Tse-tung or how I'd gotten into that mess," he said.

One day and for no reason he could explain, his memory began to slowly emerge from wherever it had been. Once all the forgotten years were reclaimed, he managed to make his way back to the United States from China where he had been since the Korean War.

And once home, he tried to reach Frank through his mother and learned from Nick Satterfield of her death. Nick had subsequently supplied him with the private phone number.

"I'm a little the worse for wear, but I speak broken Mandarin like a native," Jack said. "We're set for life at almost any Chinese restaurant in St. Louis."

Later, Jack would explain the tangled circumstances that had saved his life but prevented his identification for so many years. He had been found unconscious by a Korean peasant, who turned him over to Chinese soldiers. He didn't know why they had not either killed him or allowed nature to take its terminal course, perhaps, he told Frank, out of the expectation they could extract military information from him. "They didn't know I didn't have a clue about anything, military or personal," Jack said. "I didn't know my name and my dog tags had been lost in some frozen ditch."

Equally inexplicable, Jack added, was his harsh imprisonment in China where they at first disbelieved his amnesia and eventually forgot about him when any military information he might have had was no longer useful. He was shuttled from one imprisonment to another for several years and eventually wound up as a laborer on a large collective farm near an international border. Once his memory returned, he resolved to escape, something that would have been impossible had he not received help from a low level but highly disgruntled communist official at the farm. "It was the first luck I'd had in a long time," Jack said.

Out of China, Jack sought out a U.S. embassy, where his story was initially met with something between skepticism and disbelief until Marine Corps records were able to partially confirm his account of events. Those records, however, were unable to document his time in China, although the scars from his injuries suggested there was some truth to his incredible claim. “They’re still investigating me, and I suspect I’ll either get a medal or go to jail,” Jack said.

Jack’s father had died several years earlier but his mother - frugal person that she was – lived on and had put his money from sale of The Outpost into conservative investments with the notion he would one day return to claim it. “She didn’t seem at all surprised when I turned up on her doorstep,” Jack told Frank. “She gave me a big hug and that where the hell have you been look I used to get when I stayed out too late.”

They discussed old times at length until Frank invited Jack to Florida where he could take an extended vacation to regain his strength and perspective, which had taken a beating during his long ordeal. The essential Jack was still there, his friend perceived, but he had been inalterably changed in some respects by an incredibly difficult experience. Fully aware of those changes, Jack sought to disguise the fundamental alterations in his persona in an effort to eradicate hard memories and recapture better times.

Frank – who had recently moved into a new water-front home not far from Naples – further instructed Jack to “stay put” in St. Louis where he would be “collected and flown south” on a Peregrine Airways plane. He had planned a trip to St. Louis, where he would gather up Molly and her son for a visit to the new place. “You remember Molly Bacon, no doubt,” he said and explained that her name was now Martin and their relationship verged on the marital but had not yet gotten that far. “I’d explain it in more detail if I understood it myself," Frank added.

The next morning Frank and Bracken were at the controls of an unmarked DC-3 that Peregrine pilots called "The Party Plane." The transport had been modified for special charter flights, generally to resort destinations with wealthy passengers who wanted something larger than their own private aircraft for special occasions. For the round-trip flight, Frank had also engaged an attractive hostess, a young French woman who had served him as a stewardess for passengers as diverse as film personalities, corporate bigwigs and various royalties, what was left of them. She had been given particular instructions to treat Jack like the military hero Frank assumed he was. "I'll make him feel like General Eisenhower in Paris at the end of the war," she said.

That evening, Frank had parked his Lincoln – one he kept at the airport for his frequent visits to St. Louis – just outside the pale of a street lamp near Molly's house. Bracken and the French woman had gone off somewhere together, and Frank and Molly were scheduled to take Jack to dinner that evening. As he emerged from the car and closed the door, two men grabbed his arms and a third assailant struck the base of his skull with a blackjack that dropped him, instantly stunned, toward the pavement. Frank hung limply between the two men – who held him off the ground – as the other figure, Joe Martin, instructed them to drag him to a more isolated spot behind a hedge row. "Out of sight, out of mind," Martin said, mainly to himself.

The men, both large and obedient to Martin, dumped Frank on the damp sod, where he painfully regained his senses as Molly's former husband kicked him in the ribs with the hard toe of his boot. "We'll see how you like it," he said and kicked him again, this time with greater force. The second blow broke a rib or two, but it also aroused Frank to full consciousness and enabled him to react to Martin's next move as the two other men stood back and looked about nervously for signs of witnesses to the struggle. They were thugs of a sort, but not the professional kind.

Intent on beating Frank to death, Martin dropped to his knees and straddled him with one hand on his throat and the other clutching the blackjack. He was eager to inflict this punishment, but he couldn't resist the temptation to lavish one final taunt on what he presumed was his helpless enemy. He was about to say "Try this on for size" when Frank, who had found a baseball-size stone on the ground, struck him on a temple with all the force his strong arm could muster. Martin hovered above him for a moment, and then fell backward, instantly and apparently dead, even to the two thugs who looked on in disbelief and then fled down the dark street to their car. Frank would later seek them out and inflict retribution in the form of beatings they were not likely to forget.

"Your ex-husband is out of the picture," Frank told Molly when she answered her door and before she could comment on his disheveled appearance. He then explained in general terms what had happened – omitting the part about his original confrontation with Martin – and called the police to report the dead body on the nearby lawn. Several hours later when the authorities had completed their investigation, and Frank had gone to a hospital emergency room to have his ribs taped, he and Molly met Jack for a late super rather than their originally scheduled dinner. "A man could starve waiting for you," Jack observed, not yet aware of the evening's events.

Frank Bonner knew the limits of his considerable physical and other abilities and realized that he rather than Joe Martin could have lost his life on that suburban lawn. Had the blow from the blackjack knocked him out and allowed his assailant to finish the job, his lifeless body rather than Martin's would have been in temporary refrigeration at the coroner's office. These thoughts flowed slowly through Frank's mind – temporarily erasing awareness of his painful ribs – as he listened to Jack and Molly tell each other about their lives since high school. The dining room where they ate was empty except for the wait staff, who Frank had bribed along with a few members of the kitchen crew to remain at work beyond closing time.

Given his condition, Frank would have postponed the evening out had the conflict with Martin not turned his thoughts to the fragility of life, importance of friends and lovers as well as other clichés that only got that way through an attachment to truth. "You may have noticed my growing fondness for you," Frank said to Molly when Jack had excused himself and gone off to the men's room to relieve an organ that had been somewhat damaged during his long imprisonment.

"Pardon me," she replied, surprised by an apparent compliment that had no connection with anything he had said to her that evening and thinking, once she thought about it, that his fondness was surely the slow growing kind, given the time they had known each other.

"I love you, Molly," he added in an attempt to correct the inadequacy of his original remark, which was meant to prepare her for the decision he had made while a tired emergency room doctor had taped his ribs earlier that night. "Will you marry me?" he concluded, and watched to see if her expression would telegraph the response. It didn't, and she took a few long moments to consider the question.

"Oh, what the hell," she said at last. "Why not?"

THE END

Other Books by Dave Snyder

Mexican Summer and Other Seasons

A memoir centered in Mexico during the summer of 1950 that recalls earlier events, both personal and historical.

French Spring and its Aftermath

Still another memoir, this one commencing with a trip to Europe aboard the original Queen Mary in 1951 and continuing through most of the author's life.

The Murderous Dilemma of Bill Price

The introduction of the fictional detective, Bill Price, and the first volume in The Bill Price Trilogy.

The Deadly Transit of Toby Barnes

The second volume in The Trilogy and the one in which Bill Price tracks his principal adversary.

The Reluctant Decline of Bill Price

The final volume in The Trilogy, which easily contains as much bloodshed and trauma as the earlier books.